PRAISE FOR KE⅃

"If you're looking for a new author to read, you can't go wrong with Kellie Coates Gilbert."
~**Lisa Wingate**, NY Times bestselling author of *Before We Were Yours*

"Well-drawn, sympathetic characters and graceful language"
~**Library Journal**

"Deft, crisp storytelling"
~**RT Book Reviews**

"I devoured the book in one sitting."
~**Chick Lit Central**

"Gilbert's heartfelt fiction is always a pleasure to read."
~**Buzzing About Books**

"Kellie Coates Gilbert delivers emotionally gripping plots and authentic characters."
~**Life Is Story**

"I laughed, I cried, I wanted to throw my book against the wall, but I couldn't quit reading."
~**Amazon reader**

"I have read other books I had a hard time putting down, but this story totally captivated me."

AS THE SUN RISES

TETON MOUNTAIN SERIES
BOOK 4

KELLIE COATES GILBERT

Cover Design: Kim Killion/The Killion Group

This book is dedicated to Penny Baker.
No one could ask for a sweeter sister-in-law.

ALSO BY KELLIE COATES GILBERT

Purchase links found on my website:

www.kelliecoatesgilbert.com

TETON MOUNTAIN SERIES

Where We Belong – Book 1

Echoes of the Heart – Book 2

Holding the Dream – Book 3

As the Sun Rises – Book 4

MAUI ISLAND SERIES

Under the Maui Sky – Book 1

Silver Island Moon – Book 2

Tides of Paradise – Book 3

The Last Aloha – Book 4

Ohana Sunrise – Book 5

Sweet Plumeria Dawn – Book 6

Songs of the Rainbow – Book 7

Hibiscus Christmas – Book 8

PACIFIC BAY SERIES

Chances Are – Book 1

Remember Us – Book 2

Chasing Wind – Book 3

Between Rains – Book 4

SUN VALLEY SERIES

Sisters – Book 1

Heartbeats – Book 2

Changes – Book 3

Promises – Book 4

TEXAS GOLD COLLECTION

A Woman of Fortune – Book 1

Where Rivers Part – Book 2

A Reason to Stay – Book 3

What Matters Most – Book 4

STAND ALONE NOVELS:

Mother of Pearl

AVAILABLE AT ALL MAJOR RETAILERS

To purchase at special discounts:

www.kelliecoatesgilbertbooks.com

AS THE SUN RISES

TETON MOUNTAIN SERIES, BOOK 4

Kellie Coates Gilbert

1

Torn pieces of sunlight whispered through the pines, landing on the shattered log where Capri Jacobs sat gazing over Jenny Lake. Each lap of the water hitting the shoreline matched Capri's heartbeat—a beat she once believed sure and steady.

Capri sat on the fallen log, rested her head atop her knees, and savored the memories. How many times had they sat here together, fishing poles in hand, as the sun rose over the cragged mountaintops in the distance?

The period just after sunrise and the couple of hours before sunset were considered prime times for fishing. But it wasn't about how many trout they landed. "A day spent fishing isn't about the catch but about the peace found in the waiting," Dick often repeated.

Tears sprouted.

Capri angrily wiped them away as her phone buzzed on the log beside her. It was her mom.

"Where are you?" the text read.

Capri sighed and picked up the phone.

Crap! She was late.

She quickly tapped out a reply. "On my way."

She stood, her black high-heeled shoes wobbling slightly in the pine needles, and stuffed the phone in the pocket of her black dress before pecking her way down the winding dirt trail. Halfway to the car, her hair caught on a low limb, pulling a strand of blonde hair from her updo.

Without bothering to fix the stray piece, she made her way to her prized pickup, a bright red Dodge D150 Adventurer Lil' Red Express truck she'd brought home from an auction in Denver, all tricked out with oak wood panels, gold pin-striping over the wheel wells, and dual-chrome exhaust stacks.

In 1978, the Dodge Lil' Red Express was the fastest American-made vehicle from 0 to 100 MPH as tested by *Car and Driver* magazine—an extravagant purchase, but you only go around once on this earth.

The sentiment caught in her throat. Tears threatened yet again. Capri set her jaw determined to hold them back.

She opened the unlocked door, slipped onto the red vinyl bench seat, and jammed the key into the slot. She turned the key and started the engine sending a roar into the silence as she threw the gearshift into reverse.

Her foot jammed the gas pedal, sending the truck lurching back with enough force to pin her against the seat. Undeterred, she slammed the gearshift into the drive position and gunned the engine, sending dirt flying.

Ten minutes later, she was speeding down the highway when a flash in the rearview mirror caught her attention.

"Dammit!"

She cursed a second time as she pulled the truck to the side of the road before returning her gaze to the flashing blue lights.

Capri fumbled for her wallet and retrieved her driver's license as she watched the uniformed officer step from the police car and saunter toward her.

She unrolled the passenger window.

"Capri, you were speeding. Again."

"Sorry, Fleet. I—"

Their town deputy's brows drew together. "Why aren't you at the church?"

"I'm heading that way now."

Fleet Southcott nodded. "Okay, look—just follow me."

As he headed back to his patrol car, Capri let out a sigh of relief. She wasn't normally so lucky.

Fleet pulled out and motioned for her to follow as he turned on his lights, adding the siren for good measure. Not that there were many cars on the road at this time of the morning.

She nodded and complied, easing her truck back onto the highway behind him.

It was Dick's idea to have his memorial service in the quiet solitude of morning, believing that those who gathered to remember him at such an hour would experience the same tranquility and clarity that he found in the mornings first light, a fitting tribute to the man who found comfort in the stillness before the world awoke—especially since his grim diagnosis.

Dick also insisted on being cremated, despite her mother's protests. "Where will I visit you?" she argued.

"I don't want to be confined to one place," came his answer. "The mountains are my sanctuary, where I feel most connected to the earth and sky."

Cremation, for him, symbolized a return to the elements, allowing his essence to blend with the winds, the streams, and the rugged peaks that had always been his refuge. By being spread over the mountain area he cherished, he could remain part of the landscape that had shaped his spirit, forever intertwined with the wild beauty that had given him so much peace and inspiration.

Capri lifted her chin slightly. That would be her choice as well...when her time came.

She choked up with tears.

She used to hate him. Her stepdad wasn't the kind of guy who gave you a lot to like. He tended to get a bit mean when he drank.

Thankfully, Dick had finally sobered up years ago after his fourth car accident, where he put a young family in the hospital. The event served as the catalyst for some major changes in his life, not just in his drinking but in how he interacted with his family and friends. Soon, the old Dick gave way to a new version—a man who quietly gained the respect of others.

Capri's sight clouded as she blinked away the emotion. Dick was the only father she'd ever known.

Just before their arrival at Moose Chapel, Fleet cut his sirens and lights. She followed him into the gravel parking lot and wedged her truck between Reva's car and Albie Barton's Jeep.

"Thanks, Fleet," she said, giving the deputy a light arm punch before she made her way into the chapel.

Moose Chapel, a small rustic church nestled in the heart of Wyoming, was filled to capacity with the residents of Thunder Mountain, who had come to pay their final respects to Dick Jacobs. The wooden pews, worn smooth by generations of worshipers, were occupied by men and women whose lives Dick had touched in countless ways. Sunlight streamed through the simple open-air window at the front of the church, casting soft hues of color across the room, mingling with the scent of pine that permeated the air. The faces in the pews reflected a deep sense of loss but also a shared gratitude for having known a man whose presence had been as steadfast and enduring as the mountains that surrounded them.

Ignoring the nods of greeting and looks of sympathy, Capri found her way to the spot where her mother sat at the front and slipped in beside her. She clutched her hands in her lap.

Her mom smiled and covered her hands with her own. She squeezed tightly as Pastor Pete made his way to the podium.

Pastor Pete stood before the congregation; his voice steady yet filled with emotion as he spoke of Dick Jacobs. "Today, we gather not to mourn a loss but to celebrate a life well-lived. Dick was a man of quiet strength whose love for these mountains was as deep as the valleys they carved. He taught us the value of simplicity, of finding peace in natures embrace, and of the importance of community. Though his presence will be sorely missed, we find comfort in knowing that his spirit is now with the Lord, as free as the wind that sweeps through the Teton peaks he cherished."

Capri's ears began to ring. She struggled to swallow as her heart pounded so fiercely, she feared it might shatter her ribs.

"Breathe," she told herself. "Just breathe."

Suddenly, her chest tightened as if a vise had clamped around her lungs, making each breath shallow and desperate. Her heart raced uncontrollably, thudding against her ribcage like it was trying to escape. A wave of dizziness washed over her, and the room seemed to close in, the walls pressing closer with every second. Cold sweat trickled down her spine, and a terrifying sense of doom gripped her, overwhelming her thoughts with a flood of fear she couldn't name or control. She clutched the wooden bench, gasping, trying to ground herself in a reality that was slipping away.

Pastor Pete paused, concern sprouting on his face. "Capri? Are you alright?"

In the distance of her mind, she could hear her mother's voice. "Help! Something's wrong with my daughter!"

2

Capri stood on the front porch of Reva's cabin, lingering as the soothing rush of the nearby creek filled her ears. The sound promised a peace she desperately wished she could claim for herself.

This was the first time she and her lifelong friends had gathered for their weekly get-together since the incident at Dick's funeral—when she'd lost control and made a complete fool of herself.

Before she could even raise a hand to ring the doorbell, the heavy wooden door swung open. "There you are!" Reva exclaimed, pulling Capri into a tight embrace. "Right on time." Reva had an affinity for punctuality.

Capri followed Reva inside, joining Charlie Grace and Lila, who were already seated on the wraparound cream-colored leather sofa.

Reva's house was a showcase of mountain chic décor. Warm tones, local stone and timbers, inlays of metals, and lots of leather furnishings created an inviting interior. But even the cozy charm of Reva's home couldn't distract Capri from the way her friends looked at her when she walked in.

Their eyes met hers, filled with a sympathy Capri had no use for. She stiffened, offering a tight smile that didn't reach her eyes.

"Capri," Charlie Grace greeted, rising to give her a quick hug, her touch light as if afraid Capri might break.

Lila followed, her embrace lingering a bit longer, and Capri could almost feel the unspoken words of concern in the way her friend squeezed her arm.

"I'm fine," Capri said briskly, pulling away and waving off their worried looks. "Really. I'm already over it. Life goes on, right?"

The room was thick with unspoken words, but the tension broke as Reva, ever the hostess, moved to the kitchen with a practiced ease. "We weren't sure you'd make it," Reva said, heading for the kitchen.

"I hope everyone's hungry," Reva said, a smile tugging at her lips as she brought out a tray laden with appetizers. "I've got goat cheese-stuffed mushrooms, bacon-wrapped dates, and my famous spinach artichoke dip, fresh out of the oven." She grinned. "And before anyone asks, no I did not make them. Verna picked them up in Jackson when she ran a business errand for me."

Despite Reva's obvious intellect, her cooking skills were lacking. She'd been known to dig through the trash to reread the box instructions for mac 'n cheese.

The aroma of roasted garlic filled the cabin, mingling with the sweet, smoky scent of the bacon. Reva's spread was always a highlight of their gatherings, and despite herself, Capri felt her mood lift a fraction.

Reva set the tray on the coffee table, then turned back to retrieve a pitcher of something that looked bright and citrusy. "For cocktails tonight, I've made a grapefruit and rosemary gin fizz. Something light and refreshing."

She poured the pale pink liquid into glasses, garnishing

each with a sprig of rosemary and a twist of grapefruit peel. The drinks looked as good as they always did, vibrant and tempting.

"Except for me," Reva added, setting down her own drink—a tall glass filled with sparkling water, a splash of what was likely pomegranate juice, and a few fresh mint leaves. "You all know I'm sticking to the good stuff."

Capri reached for her glass, forcing a grin as she clinked it against Lila's. "Here's to moving on," she said, downplaying the tightness in her chest with a sip of the tart, herbaceous gin fizz. The others echoed her toast, but Capri's mind was already elsewhere, pushing away the thoughts of her stepfather and the lingering sadness she refused to let take hold.

The four women settled into their usual rhythm, chattering about everything from the latest town gossip to the upcoming Fourth of July celebration. Lila recounted a particularly amusing story about a runaway pig that had caused chaos at the farmer's market, and for a moment, the room was filled with laughter, the easy camaraderie they'd always shared.

"Love the new couch," Lila noted, running her hands across the soft leather surface. "Brave color choice for a mom with a toddler."

Reva grinned. "Yeah, I'm learning that the hard way. Let's just say I've become an expert in cleaning up juice spills and crayon masterpieces." She turned to Charlie Grace. "Speaking of messes—I heard your barn flooded in last week's downpour. Boy, that was quite the storm."

Charlie Grace nodded. "Thankfully, Gibbs showed up for once. He helped evacuate the animals and borrowed a sump pump from some guy he knew in Jackson. Had the water out in less than twenty-four hours. A bed of fresh straw did the rest."

Lila reached for one of the bacon-wrapped dates. "We had several people report the same. Thankfully, no animal issues. Just messes to clean up."

There was a brief silence before Charlie Grace exchanged glances with the others. She leaned back in her chair, hesitating for just a second before she spoke. "Capri, about the funeral…"

The lightness in the room evaporated instantly. Capri's smile faltered, and her fingers tightened around her glass. "I don't want to talk about it," she said, her voice firm.

"Capri, we're worried about you," Reva interjected softly, her eyes full of concern.

"I said I'm fine," Capri replied, her tone sharp enough to cut through the lingering tension. "It was just a moment, that's all. I'm over it."

"But you're not, and that's okay," Lila said gently, leaning forward. "We're here for you, you know that, right? You don't have to go through this alone."

Capri set her drink down with a little too much force. "I didn't come here to be analyzed. Can't we just enjoy the evening?"

"We are enjoying it," Charlie Grace said, her voice steady but filled with love. "But we care about you too much to just ignore what happened. You scared us, Capri."

Capri's gaze flicked to each of her friends in turn, seeing the worry etched on their faces. "I'm not weak," she muttered, more to herself than to them.

"Of course you're not," Reva said, her tone firm yet reassuring. "But even the strongest people need help sometimes."

Capri's defenses wavered for a moment, but she quickly rebuilt the walls around her heart. "I don't need to be coddled," she said, her declaration thick with emotion. "Not about this. We knew Dick had cancer and didn't have much time. It wasn't like this was a surprise."

"We're not coddling you," Lila assured her. "We're just… being your friends. Let us in, Capri."

The room was heavy with the weight of their unspoken

worries. Capri swallowed hard, fighting back the tears that threatened to surface. "I just...I just want to forget that incident at the church ever happened."

Charlie Grace reached out and gently took Capri's hand. "We get it. But burying it isn't the answer. Let us help you carry it, even if just a little."

Capri sighed, her shoulders slumping slightly. "I don't know if I can."

"You don't have to know," Reva said softly. "We're not going anywhere."

The words hung in the air, a promise of unwavering support, and Capri found herself nodding, even as she struggled to keep her emotions in check.

The tension slowly eased as they sat in silence, the warmth of their friendship wrapping around Capri like a soft, comforting blanket. She wasn't ready to dive into the depths of her pain, but maybe—just maybe—she didn't have to face it alone. With a deep breath, she squeezed Charlie Grace's hand and offered a small, tentative smile.

"Okay," she whispered, her voice barely audible but filled with a glimmer of acceptance.

Her friends smiled back, a silent understanding passing between them. They didn't need to say anything more; they'd be there, no matter what.

Capri leaned back in her chair, the weight on her chest lifting just enough for her to breathe easier. "Fine, we'll face it together," she said, a playful grin tugging at the corners of her mouth. "But if anyone suggests group therapy, I'm out of here."

The room erupted in laughter, the tension melting away, and Capri couldn't help but smile. "Who knew emotional breakdowns could be such a bonding experience?"

Less than twenty minutes later, Capri picked up the remainder of her second cocktail and tossed it back, emptying the stemmed glass. She stood. "Look, I hate to cut this short, but I need to get home and check on Mom."

"How's she doing?" Lila asked.

"Fine. I mean, she just lost her husband, but like I mentioned earlier, it was expected. In some ways, I think Dick's passing was a relief. It was hard for her at the end, watching him in such pain." Capri paused and took a trembling breath. "So, anyway—I'll catch you guys later." She turned her focus on Reva. "Please tell Verna those were great eats. Especially the stuffed mushrooms."

Reva smiled. "I will."

They all walked her to the door.

As soon as it closed, Reva turned to the others. "Are any of you believing this act she's putting on?"

Both Charlie Grace and Lila shook their heads. "Not for a minute."

3

Arriving home, Capri eased her truck into the yard of the small cabin she'd shared with her mother and Dick for most of her life, stopping her vehicle near a stand of pine trees shadowed by moonlight.

When questioned about her decision to live with her parents, she simply shrugged and answered. "It's free." Everyone in Thunder Mountain knew full well that cash did not weigh in as the deciding factor. Capri owned Grand Teton Whitewater Adventures. She killed it financially, especially during the heavy tourist season.

Her reasons extended far past what she was willing to explain.

Growing up, Capri was dedicated to protecting her mother. Her mom's well-being was paramount—especially back before Dick sobered up.

She was even more grateful to be close by this past year as Dick's health declined. Now, her mother would need her even more.

Capri cut the engine.

She wasn't particularly religious, but she liked to think the guy above had honored her prayers for the family she always hoped for. Now that Dick was gone, that had all changed. But she and her mom still had one another.

Unlike Reva's gorgeous cabin perched on prime property bordering the Snake River, her mother's place was small and located on a discreet parcel of land a few miles south of town, tucked among towering pines. The weathered wooden shingles on the cabin's roof, aged by years of mountain weather, extended over a simple porch where wooden beams supported an overhang. Her mom's potted flowering plants and surrounding gardens added a touch of life to the entrance.

The heart of the cabin, however, was the stone fireplace—a robust structure of large, uneven rocks, its chimney reaching proudly above the roofline.

Capri made her way to the front door, smiling at the notion her mother had left the porch light on for her.

Inside, she made her way to a well-worn plaid sofa, its cushions softened by decades of use and facing the stone fireplace, where a stack of wood lay ready to kindle a fire. Nearby, a low coffee table, scuffed from years of service, held a few well-thumbed books and a glass ashtray, despite the fact that both her mother and Dick had stopped smoking years back.

After tossing her jacket and purse on the sofa, she tip-toed down the shag-carpeted hallway to the open door of the master bedroom. Despite the bedside lamp still being on, her mother was sound asleep.

Capri pulled the comforter up and tucked it around the woman's slumbering frame. She bent and lightly kissed the top of her mom's head before stealthily backing out of the room. She closed the door behind her.

Her mother was no doubt exhausted, not having slept much in the past week. Capri had heard her up in the middle of the night several times.

After retrieving a soda from the refrigerator, she moved into the tiny living room and sank onto the sofa, letting out a long breath as she stared at the ceiling, trying to push away the ache that had settled deep in her chest. Shaking off the feeling, she grabbed for the television remote, setting the volume low so as not to wake her mom.

That's when she noticed a stack of boxes, all neatly taped up, lined against the wall like soldiers ready to be shipped out. Puzzled, she frowned and sat up. Those hadn't been there earlier. Curiosity prickled at her, pulling her off the couch and across the room.

She knelt near the stack, her fingers grazing the cardboard, feeling the smooth edges of the tape. A wave of unease washed over her. With a slow, deliberate motion, Capri peeled back the tape of the nearest box, her heart thudding in her chest. She lifted the flaps and was immediately met with a familiar scent, the one that clung to Dick's old jackets and flannel shirts—a mixture of pine, woodsmoke, and something uniquely him.

Capri frowned. Why were Dick's things packed away so soon?

Inside a second box she found his worn leather gloves, the ones he always wore while chopping wood, the tips of the fingers frayed. Beneath them was his favorite thermos, still dented from that time he'd slipped on the ice last winter. There was the tattered fly-fishing guidebook he swore by, pages dog-eared and stained from years of use. Capri's breath hitched when she noticed a small, framed photograph tucked into the corner—her and Dick standing side by side in front of the cabin, smiling wide after a long day of fishing.

Her mother had packed all of this away, stowed it out of sight as if Dick had never existed, as if the man who had been a father to Capri, who had been a rock for both of them, could be erased with the sealing of a box. The realization hit her like a punch to the gut, followed quickly by a surge of anger. How could her mother be so quick to flush him from their lives?

Capri's fists clenched as she closed the box, the sound of the cardboard folding back into place loud in the silence of the room.

As Capri stood there, struggling with a mix of emotions, she heard the soft creak of the floorboards behind her. She turned to see her mother standing in the doorway, her expression weary but calm, as if she had expected this confrontation.

"Mom," Capri began, her voice steady but laced with an edge. "Why did you pack up Dick's things already? It hasn't even been a week. Why rush to erase him from the house?"

Her mother's eyes softened with a sadness that Capri wasn't prepared for. "Capri, honey, it's not about erasing him," she said quietly, stepping into the room. "It's just... it's too painful to see his things every day. Every time I walk past his chair or his fishing gear, it feels like a knife in my heart. I can't keep living with these constant reminders, not right now. It's just too hard."

Capri's heart pulled at the sight of her mother's vulnerability, but the resentment still gnawed at her. She wanted to argue, to insist that this wasn't right, that they couldn't just box him up like he was a piece of old furniture. But seeing the grief etched in her mother's face, Capri found herself swallowing her anger.

"I get it, Mom," she said, her tone softening but still firm. "I understand it hurts, but..." She paused, struggling to keep her face from showing what she was feeling inside. "Look, I'll load them in the truck tomorrow morning and take them away."

Her mother nodded, relief flickering in her eyes. "Thank you, Capri. I just need some space... some time to breathe."

Capri forced a small smile and nodded, though inside, her resolve was solidifying. "I'll take care of it," she promised. As she watched her mother leave the room, her mind was already made up. She wasn't about to let Dick's memory be thrown out. Tomorrow, she'd take those boxes to Grand Teton Whitewater Adventures, where she'd find a safe place to store them.

4

Capri pulled her red truck into the gravel lot of Grand Teton Whitewater Adventures, the familiar sound of tires crunching against the rocks filling the quiet morning air. She glanced at the rearview mirror, taking in the pile of boxes stacked neatly in the truck bed. A sigh escaped, a mix of exhaustion and determination.

She had a busy day ahead and now had to deal with finding a place for these boxes that would be out of the way—at least until she was ready to go through the items. There were things she'd no doubt like to keep. Even if her mom couldn't bear to look at Dick's belongings, all Capri had left were her memories and his stuff.

The best place might be one of the bays in the back where they stored extra rafts, kayaks, and paddles.

As she stepped out of the truck, early morning sun glinted through the nearby aspen trees that lined the river, casting long shadows across the parking lot. The cool mountain breeze caught her hair, whipping it around her face. She tucked a few loose strands behind her ear and headed toward the back, ready to start unloading.

"Hey, Cap!" a voice called out, drawing her attention to the lanky figure strolling out from the office. The familiar nickname signaled the voice belonged to Bodhi West, one of her employees. He sauntered over with a relaxed grin, his long brown hair falling in casual waves around his tanned face. He wore a faded REI T-shirt and cargo shorts that had seen better days, the kind of outfit that might've been new once upon a time, but now had the worn-in, lived-in look of someone who spent more time outdoors than indoors.

"Bodhi," Capri greeted. "Give me a hand with these, will you?"

"Sure thing, boss," he replied, moving to the back of the truck with the kind of ease that came from someone who didn't exactly rush through life. He grabbed a box, balancing it effortlessly on one arm. "You know, these early morning shifts are starting to grow on me."

Capri rolled her eyes with a smirk. "That's because your morning routine consists of rolling out of bed and into the truck. Real tough."

He chuckled, unfazed by her jab. They carried the first set of boxes together to the designated storage area, the small talk flowing easily between them. Once inside, Capri set her box down with a slight grunt, wiping the dust from her hands on her jeans.

After several trips, she turned to him. "Thanks for the help," she said, brushing her hands off. "You can head back to—"

Bodhi's phone buzzed loudly, interrupting her. He glanced at the screen, a wide grin spreading across his face. "Hold on a sec," he said, stepping toward the door. "It's my girl in Seattle. She's coming to visit soon."

"Sure," Capri replied, her voice flat as she watched him slip outside, the door creaking slightly behind him. She stood there for a moment, letting the quiet of the storage area settle around her. The place smelled of old wood, dusty aluminum, and the faint scent of river water, a comforting scent that usually grounded her.

But today, her thoughts were elsewhere. Capri's gaze drifted to the open box beside her. Without thinking, she reached over to close it, but her hand froze as she spotted the familiar cover of a collection of *Gilmore Girls* DVDs. A small gasp escaped her lips, and she felt a sharp pang in her chest. Memories flooded back—late nights with Dick, curled up on the couch, laughing and talking as they watched episode after episode. He had given her that box set for her birthday years ago, a gift that had meant more to her than he'd probably ever realized.

Her fingers hovered over the DVDs for a moment longer before she quietly pulled them from the box. She didn't say a word, didn't let herself think too much about it. Instead, she turned on her heel and headed back to her truck. The DVDs landed on the passenger seat with a soft thud.

Capri's breath hitched as a memory formed. She was in grade school, just before her mother married Dick, and Willie McKee, the town's new bully, had made the mistake of taunting her in front of everyone. "Hey, Capri! Where's your daddy? Oh, right—you don't have one!" he'd sneered, his voice dripping with cruelty.

The sting of his words hit harder than she'd expected, and before she knew it, she'd launched herself at him with a ferocity that shocked even her. She remembered the sound of fists meeting flesh, the way the playground had fallen silent except for Willie's cries.

"Take it back! Take it back!" she'd yelled, her voice raw with a pain she didn't understand at the time.

It wasn't until Charlie Grace, Lila, and Reva pulled her off him, their faces pale with shock, that she realized the entire playground had been watching. She'd gotten grounded for her outburst when the teacher found out, but in her heart, she knew it had been worth it.

She hadn't just beaten Willie that day; she'd fought against the deep-seated loneliness that had followed her for as long as she could remember, the fear that she wasn't worth sticking around for.

What did it say that her real dad had left and never bothered to return?

That question had haunted her, gnawing at her self-worth, making her feel like she had to prove she was strong enough to stand on her own. Beating Willie wasn't just about silencing his taunts; it was about silencing the doubts inside her, the ones that whispered she wasn't enough, that she didn't belong. Even now, those doubts chased her, driving her to push harder, to take risks, to show the world—and herself—that she could survive, no matter who had left her behind.

Yes, her heart was in pieces right now. But she'd find a way to survive this.

Capri closed the truck door with a decisive click, taking a deep breath before heading back to the office, ready to tackle the rest of the day. After checking incoming emails and phone messages, she rejoined Bodhi outside.

Capri moved for the garage doors of the main building and yanked them open. Inside the aluminum and wooden structure, where the rafts and gear were stored, was a mix of rugged functionality and organized chaos.

The walls were lined with sturdy wooden shelves, each one sagging slightly under the weight of coiled ropes, helmets, and paddles, their bright colors standing out against the rough-hewn wood. The floor was scuffed and worn, bearing the marks of years of heavy boots and dripping wet gear, with a faint smell of rubber, river water, and the earthy scent of damp wood hanging in the air. In the center of the space, multiple massive rafts were propped up on metal racks, their faded exteriors bearing the scars of countless journeys down the treacherous rivers. The high ceiling, crisscrossed with exposed beams, gave the room a cavernous feel, the light filtering in through small, grimy windows casting long shadows over the equipment.

Despite the disorder, everything had its place, a testament to the countless hours spent here preparing for the unpredictable adventures ahead.

Bodhi sauntered over, stretching lazily as he approached the stack of gear. "Ready to load up, boss?"

Capri shot him a look, her voice edged with a tinge of impatience. "Let's get moving. We've got a long day ahead."

They moved with practiced ease, securing two rafts to the company trailer, tying down the life vests and paddles. Capri's hands were steady, but her mind was anything but. She was the owner, the boss, the one who knew these rivers better than anyone. But today, they weren't here for the tourists or the thrill-seekers. Today was about testing the water—literally. The spring thaw had swollen the rivers to near-dangerous levels, and she needed to ensure their routes were safe. At least, that was the reason she told herself.

As they drove toward the river, Bodhi leaned back, a casual grin on his face. "So, why the sudden need to 'test' the water? Don't we have guides for that?"

Capri kept her eyes on the road, her knuckles white against the steering wheel. "The Snake River's been unpredictable this year. I want to see it for myself."

In truth, she needed the rush. The way the water could rip you apart or cradle you in its currents—it matched the chaos inside her head.

When they arrived at the riverbank, the Snake River snarled ahead of them. The water churned, dark and fast. The air was thick with the scent of wet earth and fresh pine, a combination that usually brought Capri peace. But today, it only fueled the fire within her.

"Capri, are you sure about this?" Bodhi's voice had lost its earlier levity, replaced with concern. He could see the danger in the water, the way the rapids twisted and turned, foaming white against the jagged rocks. "Make sure we stick to the left channel. Reports coming in say it's a bit tamer."

Capri ignored him, dragging the first raft toward the water. "Got it." She turned to him, her voice challenging. "You can sit it out if you want. But, I need to check the runs, just like I do every year. It's the job."

Bodhi hesitated, watching her with a mixture of worry and disbelief. "Well, Cap. I ain't letting you go alone. The rapids are wicked, and the water's running high—"

"Just load the raft, Bodhi," Capri snapped, her voice cutting through the roar of the river.

As they launched into the river, the water moved with a steady, almost deceptive calm, its surface rippling gently under the early morning light. The current was strong but not yet menacing, carrying the raft forward with a sense of purpose.

Overhead, an eagle soared, its wings outstretched against the clear sky, casting a fleeting shadow on the water below.

The riverbank slipped away behind them, the aspen trees lining the shore swaying slightly in the breeze as if bidding them farewell.

As the raft glided smoothly down the river, Bodhi relaxed a little, leaning back as he dipped his paddle into the water with easy strokes. "Not so bad after all," he said, flashing Capri a grin. "I was thinking you were leading us straight into the jaws of death."

Capri smirked, her eyes on the horizon. "Don't get too comfortable, Bodhi. The river's just being polite right now. It'll show its true colors soon enough."

He chuckled, shaking his head. "You always gotta be so dramatic, Cap? Maybe this time we'll get lucky."

Capri's smile faded slightly as she murmured, "Luck can often be fickle."

As they continued downriver, the gentle current gradually

began to shift, the once calm waters now starting to bubble and churn with increasing energy. The trees along the banks thinned out, giving way to jagged rocks jutting out from the shore, and the soothing sound of the river was replaced by the distant roar of rapids.

Capri's grip on the paddle tightened, her gaze sharpening as she scanned the turbulent water ahead. The air grew cooler, and the sun dipped behind a cloud, casting a shadow over the river, as if warning them of the challenge that lay just around the bend.

Suddenly, the raft surged forward, caught in the grip of the current. Capri's hands clenched the paddle even more, her muscles tense, her mind focused on the treacherous path ahead.

"Hold on, Bodhi. Here we go!" she yelled over the roar of the water.

The first rapid hit like a freight train, the water slamming against the raft, jerking it sideways. Capri's heart pounded in her chest, but she didn't flinch. She powered through, her paddle blade digging into the churning water, forcing the raft forward.

Bodhi's voice cut through the chaos, yelling over the roar of the rapids. "Capri! Left! Take the left channel!"

But she was beyond listening. Yes, the right channel was narrower, rockier—deadlier, but she was a highly skilled raft guide. She had this. And that was where she was going.

The world around her blurred, the river and the sky merging into one angry, relentless force. The smell of wet earth and the metallic tang of the water filled her senses as she pushed forward, determined to conquer the river, to prove to herself that she could still control something, anything.

The raft careened toward the rocks, and for a moment, the world tilted dangerously. Bodhi's shouts grew more frantic, but Capri's focus was razor-sharp. She wasn't just fighting the river

—she was fighting everything. The loss of her stepfather, the way her life was spiraling out of control, the fear that she was secretly losing herself.

She'd ridden through so many changes lately. Her close-knit group of girlfriends, once inseparable, seemed to be moving forward in ways that left her feeling unmoored. Charlie Grace was deep into a new relationship with talk of a possible wedding ahead. Reva had thrown herself into a new relationship, along with motherhood, and Lila, despite her struggles, had found love again. They were all evolving, their lives shifting like the currents of the river, while Capri felt stuck—caught in some invisible undertow that she couldn't name.

It wasn't just about the loss of her stepfather or the sudden weight of caring for her grieving mother; it was a deeper, gnawing sense that while everyone else was forging ahead, she was trapped in a place where she couldn't even see the path forward. She was surrounded by change, yet rooted in the same old patterns, unsure of how to break free from the trap inside her head.

The raft scraped against a jagged boulder, the impact jarring Capri to her core. But she held on, her knuckles white, her teeth gritted. The water surged around them, wild and unforgiving, and for a heartbeat, Capri thought they might actually make it through unscathed.

But then the river reared up again, a massive wave crashing over the side, nearly flipping the raft. Capri was thrown forward, barely holding on as the water tried to rip her away.

"Capri! We need to bail out! Now!" Bodhi's voice was desperate, but Capri was beyond reason.

She tightened her clutch on the paddle, her jaw set in grim determination. "I'm not quitting," she hollered, directing the path of the raft with all the strength she could muster, her muscles burning with the effort.

The roar of the rapids drowned out everything but the

pounding of her heart as she fought against the surging water. "Not now, not ever," she added, her voice fierce as she steered the raft toward the wildest part of the current, refusing to be overpowered by the river—or by the chaos in her life.

The river thundered in response, the final rapid ahead looming like a monster. The water foamed, the rocks below just waiting to tear them apart. But Capri didn't care. She was going to ride this out, no matter what.

As the raft plunged into the final descent, Capri felt a twisted sense of calm. The danger, the adrenaline, the sheer force of nature—it all mirrored the chaos inside her. She might not be able to control her life, but she could control this moment. She would face the rapids, the danger, the pain, and come out the other side, even if it tore her apart in the process.

And then, with a final, bone-jarring crash, the raft burst through the last rapid, the water calming around them as they drifted into the slower current. Capri was drenched, her heart pounding, but she was still there. Still fighting.

Bodhi was panting, his face pale. "You're crazy, you know that?" His anxiety-stricken expression softened into a faint grin as he shook out his soaked hair.

Capri didn't answer. She just stared at the river, her breath coming in ragged gasps, the chaos inside her still swirling, but quieter now.

The river's fury had taken its toll, but she'd won this one.

She turned to Bodhi. "Yeah, I might just be."

5

Reva adjusted her glasses, peering into the computer camera from her recently renovated mayor's office, the faint scent of fresh paint still lingering in the air. The glow of her desk lamp illuminated the room, casting a warm, inviting light that did little to hide her determined expression. "Okay, ladies, can everyone hear me?" she asked, her voice slightly distorted by the less-than-perfect Zoom connection. Small mountain towns had their advantages, but internet service wasn't always one of them.

Lila nodded, the loose ponytail she wore a rare sign of relaxation amid her usually hectic schedule "Loud and clear, Reva. What's up that couldn't wait for our Friday night get-together?"

Charlie Grace appeared next on the screen, her backdrop the rustic wooden walls of the lodge out at Teton Trails. She was holding a clipboard in one hand and a pen in the other. "I'm here, but only because I promised to be. The guests are about to head out on a trail ride, so let's make this quick."

Reva's gaze darted to the last empty square. "We're just waiting for Capri."

Just as Reva finished speaking, Capri's image popped onto the screen. Her expression was one of pure annoyance, her background a blur of outdoor scenery as she sat in the cab of her truck. "You know I hate this online nonsense. Couldn't we have met in person? Maybe catch a beer down at the Rustic Pine or something?"

Reva studied Capri's image, then frowned with concern. "You okay, Capri? You look like you just climbed out of bed."

Capri quickly waved off the comment. "No, just came in off the river, that's all." She tucked a damp hair strand behind her ear. "I'm fine."

Charlie Grace's expression filled with alarm. "This early? But the water's running really high right now."

Capri simply shrugged off the comment. "Yeah, I noticed," Capri said with a nonchalant grin. "Nothing I couldn't handle. You know me—I like a good challenge."

Reva stifled her own concern and continued, focusing on the issue at hand. "Well, I know you're all busy, so let me move on to the reason for this meeting. As you know, I am heading up this summer's Vacation Bible School and need your help to finalize the details." She grinned. "Nearly two dozen kids have registered, and more are expected. With the event less than ten days away, there's still a long list of items to do to get ready. Pastor Pete and Annie are counting on us."

Capri rolled her eyes. "I don't know why you roped me into this, Reva. You know I'm not the 'arts and crafts' type."

Charlie Grace laughed. "You're definitely not the 'sit still in front of a screen' type either, judging by how much you're squirming."

"I'm on my phone," Capri protested, holding up the device for proof.

"Whoa...hold that thing still. You're giving us all motion sickness!" Lila chimed in. "We each have our strengths, Capri.

Maybe you can be in charge of the outdoor activities. You know, something with a bit more...action."

Capri huffed but didn't argue. "Fine. But I'm not gluing anything to anything."

Reva nodded, satisfied. "Perfect. Lila, you can handle the snacks, and Charlie Grace, you're on decoration duty. And we have the Knit Wit ladies all offering to help."

Charlie Grace's eyes widened. "Decorations? I thought this was being held outdoors?"

"Exactly, but we're going with a Noah's Ark theme this year. We'll need all that goes with that. So, put your thinking hats on," Reva quipped. A sly smile crossed her face. "I know it's a big ask, but I'll need your supply list by tomorrow morning. Pastor Pete promised to round up whatever we require, including lumber to build an ark. I've already arranged for a couple of guys from my AA meeting to help with the construction."

Lila leaned forward, her voice a bit softer. "I think it's going to be fun. The kids will love it, and it's a good way to give back to the community. Count me in, and Camille will be home from college in a couple of days and can help too."

Capri crossed her arms, as if still unconvinced. "As long as it doesn't turn into one of those over-the-top productions. Keep it simple."

That brought a chuckle from Charlie Grace. "We're talking about Reva here. She never does anything simple."

Reva frowned. "Hey—" Before she could continue, the screen suddenly wobbled, the images of the women shaking slightly.

Lila gasped. "Whoa, did you feel that?"

Charlie Grace fumbled and dropped her pen, eyes wide. "Was that an earthquake?"

Capri raised an eyebrow, her irritation momentarily replaced with a look of curiosity. "Appears so."

Reva placed a hand on her desk, steadying herself as the tremor subsided. "It's been a while since we've felt any seismic activity this far south of Yellowstone."

Lila frowned. "Maybe it was the Teton Fault line. You know it follows the baseline of the mountain range. Of course, it's been hundreds of years since any activity."

Charlie Grace shrugged. "Or maybe it's just a sign that Capri should embrace technology. The earth's literally shaking to get you on board, Capri," she teased.

Capri rolled her eyes in response. "Or it's a sign that we should stop having these Zoom meetings. Before the mountains decide to tumble down on us."

A second vibration shook, much smaller this time—but noticeable, nonetheless.

"Whoa, there it goes again," Capri noted.

Just as the tremor subsided, Reva's highly strung assistant, Verna Billingsley, burst into the office, her eyes wide with alarm. "Mayor, are you alright? Should we evacuate? I already pulled the emergency protocol!" She waved a document high over her head.

Reva stifled a grin, glancing back at the screen where her friends were chuckling with amusement. "Thank you, Verna. But unless the mountain decides to walk into town for a coffee, I think we're safe—for now."

6

The tremors were the talk of the town. Especially in the Rustic Pine later that afternoon.

By the time Capri pushed through the old wooden door, the place was already buzzing with animated chatter, the kind that seemed to vibrate through the worn floorboards just like the earth had that morning.

Pastor Pete was huddled near the counter, a concerned look on his usually placid face, while Annie stood beside him, wiping down the bar with a towel. "While not big when compared to a lot of the earthquakes up north, we haven't had a strong tremor like that in a while."

Annie flung the damp towel over her shoulder. "Well, I don't think we should worry about it. We live in an area prone to earthquakes. I suppose it's inevitable we'll feel the earth move a little from time to time."

Over in the corner, the Knit Wit ladies—Oma, Betty, and Dorothy—were knitting with a fervor that suggested the very act might somehow steady the ground beneath them.

Oma looked up from her needles, a wistful smile on her face. "When it happened, I was having breakfast with Earl. I told him, 'Well, Earl, if the earth's shaking, maybe it's just Heaven's way of reminding us that you and the saints are keeping an eye on things up there.'"

Oma was a widow and often spent mornings up at the cemetery, where she routinely sat in a lawn chair next to where her beloved Earl was buried, with a platter of freshly baked cinnamon rolls and a thermos of coffee.

Albie Barton, the town's self-proclaimed intrepid reporter, was perched on a stool, his notepad already half-full of scribbled notes.

Capri slid into a seat at the bar, catching Albie's eye. "Let me guess," she said with a smirk. "Your headline tomorrow will be something like 'Thunder Mountain Rumbles: Is the Big One Coming?'"

Albie chuckled, tapping his pen against the pad. "You're not far off, Capri. But don't forget the subhead: 'Local Residents Brace for Impact.'"

Dorothy leaned in, her voice barely above a whisper. "You don't really think it's a sign of something worse, do you, Albie?"

Before Albie could answer, Earl Dunlop piped up from across the room. "I told you, it's those fracking folks out in the Powder River Basin! I read about it—causes all sorts of problems underground."

Dorothy nodded vigorously, her needles clicking at a rapid pace. "That's right! I've heard about it too. Shakes things up like nobody's business."

Capri rolled her eyes, taking a sip of the lemonade she'd ordered. "Or maybe it's just the earth being the earth. Sometimes things just happen."

The town's conspiracy theorist, Larry York, turned his bar stool to face the others. "It's highly likely the government is conducting underground military experiments. We should start a petition to get answers from the mayor's office."

31

Pastor Pete cleared his throat, his deep voice cutting through the room. "Let's not jump to worrying and wild conjecture. There's no need to assume the worst. The good Lord has us in the palm of his hand, regardless of the earth shaking a little." He draped his arm around his wife's shoulder, pulling Annie close. "More than likely, the level of activity of the fault was a good thing. In theory, an active fault that has more frequent smaller earthquakes is less likely to have a major earthquake. The reasoning is that the pressure in the fault is being released in small doses more frequently, as opposed to being built up and finally releasing in a large earthquake. The Teton Fault is still considered active and has not had a major earthquake in recorded human history, so it would fall into this category."

Betty, who'd been silent until now, looked up from her knitting with a mischievous glint in her eye. "Well, I'll tell you this much—I'm just glad I've got plenty of yarn. If the earth swallows us up, at least I'll go out with a warm scarf."

The room erupted in laughter, a welcome break from the tension that had been building. Capri shook her head, smiling at the Knit Wit ladies. "Leave it to you three to find the silver lining in an earthquake."

Dorothy wasn't so easily soothed, though. "But what if it's not just a tremor? What if it's a warning? The Bible talks about signs, you know. Maybe we should all be preparing for something bigger."

Capri placed a reassuring hand on Dorothy's arm. "Dorothy, we're all in this together, whatever it is. Besides, if the big one's coming, I'm pretty sure Pastor Pete here would've gotten a direct memo from upstairs."

Pastor Pete grinned, shaking his head. "I don't think I'm quite that high up the chain, Capri."

Albie flipped his notepad closed, surveying the room with a journalist's eye. "All I know is this will make for one heck of a story. People are going to want to know what's happening, and it's my job to tell them."

Oma leaned over, pointing her knitting needle at him. "You make sure you tell them that we're a resilient bunch here in Thunder Mountain. We're not about to let a little shaking get the better of us."

"Darn right," Betty added. "Like I said, we'll knit our way through it if we have to."

The laughter that followed was louder this time, the kind that lifted spirits and made everyone feel a little bit safer, if only for a moment. Capri looked around at the familiar faces, feeling a surge of affection for this quirky little town.

The past few weeks had been the hardest of her life, a relentless storm that threatened to pull her under. Capri was unraveling, the weight of losing Dick too much to bear, and no one in this bar truly understood the depth of her struggle to adjust. Or, why.

The panic attack she'd endured, the crazy risks she'd taken on the river—when safety was always paramount to her nature and business—were all signs of a woman falling apart. Yet, as she sat among these familiar faces, surrounded by the warm hum of chatter and laughter, she couldn't ignore the truth that began to surface.

Despite her loss, she still had much to be thankful for—including this community of people who'd known her since grade school and had been there for her in every season of life.

Whatever shook Thunder Mountain—be it the ground beneath them or the uncertainties that loomed over them—Capri knew they'd stand together, steady as the peaks that surrounded them.

And perhaps, just perhaps, that knowledge would be what helped her find her footing again, a small but vital step toward reclaiming peace in the midst of her turmoil. She wasn't whole yet, not by a long shot, but for the first time in weeks, she could feel a sliver of hope threading through her pain.

7

Capri pulled into the yard of her home, the familiar crunch of gravel under her tires. As she stepped out of her red truck, she spotted her mother kneeling in the front flower garden, her sun hat casting a wide brim of shade over her face.

The sight warmed Capri's heart but also carried a twinge of sadness. Her mother had been through so much lately. If Capri's own heart ached this deeply after losing Dick, she could hardly fathom the depth of her mother's pain.

"Hey, Mom," Capri greeted as she walked over, her boots kicking up dust on the pathway leading to the porch. Her mother looked up, a smile breaking across her face.

"Hi, sweetheart," she replied, brushing dirt from her hands. "That was quite the tremor."

"Yeah, sure was. I mean, it wasn't all that big in terms of the Richter Scale, but it shook up the folks in town, that's for sure." She recounted the aftermath she'd encountered at the Rustic Pine. "It was the excitement of the morning. Everyone was chattering about it, sharing their opinions."

Her mother plucked a weed that had dared to grow next to

her stand of daisies. "Well, the tremors got Fuzz Lightyear all riled up earlier—scared him nearly to death."

A nostalgic smile tugged at her mother's lips. "I remember when you named him that. It was during your *Toy Story* phase. Remember how obsessed you were with that movie?"

Capri chuckled. "I sure do. I even begged Dick to build me a cardboard spaceship."

Capri's mother laughed, her eyes softening with the memory. "Privately, I asked him not to. I was afraid you might climb up on the roof with it and try to fly."

"I like to think I was adventurous."

Her mom shook her head. "More like a handful." She stretched, wincing slightly, her hand pressing against her lower back. "Ugh, getting old is no picnic," she muttered.

Capri quickly bent down, picked up the trowel and continued the task. "You do enough kneeling in this garden to make a nun jealous," she teased. "Let me finish this up for you."

Her mother pointed to a cluster of flowers, smiling. "See those hollyhocks? They're going to be stunning this summer if the deer don't make a buffet out of them."

Capri was about to reply when her mother suddenly glanced at her watch and her eyes widened in alarm. "Oh heavens, I'm late!"

"For what?" Capri asked, watching as her mother hurried to her feet.

"I'm going out to dinner with a friend," her mother tossed over her shoulder as she rushed inside, leaving Capri blinking in surprise.

"Dinner out?" Capri echoed, stunned. She was thrilled that her mother was taking her advice to get out more. She'd spent months in this house nursing Dick. It would do her good to go have some fun.

Capri finished up in the garden, tidying the tools and wiping her hands on her jeans before carrying the basket inside. She headed to the kitchen for a glass of lemonade when her mother reappeared, looking unexpectedly radiant. She wore a light blue dress that flowed around her in soft waves, cinched at the waist with a dainty belt. Her silver hair was pinned back elegantly, and she had a sparkle in her eye that Capri hadn't seen in months.

"Is that new, Mom?" Capri asked, eyebrows raised.

Her mother blushed slightly, smoothing down the front of the dress. "Yes, it is."

"And perfume?" Capri caught the subtle scent of something floral and fresh. "Since when do you wear perfume?"

Before her mother could respond, the sound of an engine cutting off outside was followed by a car door slamming shut. Her mother glanced in the mirror, suddenly flustered, and dabbed at her lipstick. "How do I look?" she asked, turning to Capri with a nervous smile.

Capri's confusion only grew, but she smiled back. "As pretty as ever."

A firm knock sounded on the door, making them both jump. "Honey, get that, please," her mother said, her voice a touch breathless as she put on the finishing touches of her lipstick.

Capri walked to the door and opened it, only to find herself face-to-face with Earl Dunlop, the large, burly man who ran the county's snow removal fleet. He wore a crisp button-down shirt and a sheepish grin.

"What are you doing here, Earl?" Capri asked, blinking at the sight of him all dressed up.

He beamed at her, his grin widening to a boyish smile that seemed out of place on his grizzled face. "I'm here to take your mama out. On a date!"

Capri stared at him, her mouth falling open in disbelief. Her mother was dating Earl Dunlop? The old guy with the kitten?

As the realization sank in, a tight knot formed in her stomach; the unexpected turn leaving her completely unsettled.

Capri turned sharply, her eyes narrowing as she faced her mother. "I don't get it, Mom. It's only been weeks since Dick died, and you're already dating?" she demanded, her voice edged with both shock and hurt.

Her mother met Capri's gaze calmly, a hint of a smile tugging at her lips. "Oh, sweetheart," she said gently. "Grief doesn't come with a schedule. And besides, I'm not dead—just a widow with a closet full of pretty dresses that need a night out. Life's too short to sit around waiting for the flowers to wilt."

Minutes later, Capri stood at the doorway, watching as Earl helped her mother into his truck, her laughter floating back on the warm summer breeze.

Capri's chest tightened with a mix of anger and disbelief. She should have seen this coming—her mother had never been one to go long without a man by her side.

But...Earl Dunlop?

Frustrated, she spun on her heel and marched to the kitchen, dumping her untouched lemonade into the sink with a splash. Yanking open the refrigerator, she grabbed a beer, popped the top, and took a long, determined gulp. She snatched another from the fridge on her way to the living room, where she rifled through the DVDs, pulled out the *Gilmore Girls* collection she'd retrieved from Dick's things, and slammed one into the player.

As the familiar theme music filled the room, she folded into the cushions on the worn sofa and muttered, "Even Stars Hollow couldn't top this Emily Gilmore nightmare."

8

In the days that followed, Capri did what she always did and buried her feelings by staying busy.

She threw herself into the frenetic pace of preparing for the rafting season, the steady hum of activity at Grand Teton Whitewater Adventures becoming her refuge from the chaos inside her.

She was the first one at the base every morning, long before the sun kissed the tips of the Tetons, unlocking the storage shed and checking the inventory of life vests, helmets, and paddles. The smell of neoprene and the crispness of the early June air became her constant companions as she meticulously inspected each raft, ensuring they were ready to brave the icy rapids.

She moved with purpose, her mind on anything but her mother, who had stunned Capri by dating so soon after Dick's death. Capri focused on the tangible, like the fraying ropes that needed replacing or the rust on the trailer hitch that needed a good sanding, finding solace in the physicality of the work.

Bodhi West ambled over as she wrestled a stubborn patch onto a worn inflatable. "You know, I can handle some of that," he offered with a grin, pushing his long hair out of his face. Capri barely glanced up, her hands steady on the repair kit. "I've got this, Bodhi. But, there's a list a mile long if you're looking for something to do." She didn't mean to sound curt, but the work gave her a sense of control she couldn't afford to lose.

Bodhi shrugged and headed toward the equipment shed, whistling a tune that grated on her nerves, though she couldn't say why. She knew he was trying to help, but Capri wasn't ready to delegate or slow down—not with the season looming and certainly not with her tangled emotions threatening to unwind her.

The days blurred together as Capri pushed herself to the limit, organizing training sessions for the summer guides and running safety drills on the still-cold river. The office phone rang off the hook with bookings. Though she had people hired to maintain the trip schedules, Capri often picked up and handled many of the calls with professional ease, her voice steady and reassuring. In the evenings, she reviewed the route maps, plotting out the safest paths for tourists and noting the danger spots where the spring runoff made the rapids especially treacherous. She even updated the website, adding new photos and highlighting the thrill of their most challenging routes.

Every task, every detail, was a distraction, a way to keep her thoughts from wandering to her mother's unexpected relationship and the gaping void Dick's death had left in her heart. But even as she busied herself, a small part of Capri knew she couldn't keep running from her feelings forever.

No matter how many tasks she completed or how many hours she spent working, she couldn't entirely escape the thoughts that crept in during quiet moments—the image of her mother moving on, the life they once had with Dick slipping further into the past.

It was a fragile balance, keeping her emotions in check, one she maintained with stubborn determination. But all it took was a single moment, an unexpected encounter, to shatter that precarious equilibrium. Like the day she caught sight of Earl holding her mother's hand in the Western Drug and General store.

Capri froze in the narrow aisle, her breath catching in her throat as she watched the two of them, their fingers intertwined like they'd been doing this for years.

The small-town grocery store slash pharmacy had a distinct charm, its mismatched shelves crammed with everything from bottles of liniment oil sitting next to marshmallows and tomato soup. The scent of aged wood and freshly baked bread mingled in the air, and Capri could almost hear the distant hum of the old fluorescent lights that flickered overhead.

She ducked behind a display of cereal boxes, peeking through a gap between the Frosted Flakes and Raisin Bran, her heart pounding.

Her mother and Earl were oblivious to her presence, their voices a low murmur as they picked out produce; their casual closeness sending a pang of betrayal through Capri's chest. Then she heard it.

The L word.

Capri nearly choked on her own breath. Something twisted deep inside her as she edged closer, pretending to examine a row of canned peaches, straining to hear their conversation. Surely, she was mistaken.

Her mother laughed softly at something Earl said, a sound Capri hadn't heard in months, and it was completely disconcerting. She hated feeling like a voyeur, but she couldn't pull herself away, couldn't reconcile the image of her mother being so at ease with another man when the loss of Dick was still so raw for Capri.

Earl picked up her mother's hand and kissed the back of it. Her mom let out a giggle filled with delight.

Capri's heart thudded against her chest. She'd believed those days were far behind her, but now, every childhood memory felt fresh—each faceless man passing through their lives like a reopened wound on her heart. She may have been just a little girl, but at this moment, she vividly recalled the unfamiliar faces at their dinner table and in her mother's bedroom.

When Dick first came into their lives, he brought along dolls for Capri and a love for Monopoly that quickly won her over. She liked him, finding comfort in his playful nature and easygoing presence. She finally had a daddy.

But then the drinking started, and those early days of warmth faded into a blur of broken promises and shouting. However, the last couple of decades had been a different story. Dick had gotten sober, and they had finally become the family she had always longed for, creating a bond that healed old wounds and gave her the father figure she needed.

Capri startled out of her thoughts when her mother caressed Earl's beard.

Capri couldn't stand it one more second. She straightened, determined to walk away. At least until they were home, and Capri could confront her mother and talk some sense into her.

But then, just as Capri thought she might escape unnoticed, a loud, nasally voice cut through the air like a knife. "Well, if it isn't Capri Jacobs! Sneaking around, are we?"

Capri's blood ran cold as she turned to find Nicola Cavendish standing there, her hands planted on her hips, a satisfied smirk curling her lips. Nicola was the town's self-appointed purveyor of gossip, her tongue sharp and unforgiving. And she wasn't about to let Capri off the hook.

"Spying on your mama, are you?" Nicola continued, her voice rising with every word, drawing the attention of everyone in the store. "It's not every day you see a grown woman hiding behind a box of Cap'n Crunch. What's the matter, Capri? Not happy that your mama's moving on?"

Capri's face burned with embarrassment, but before she could respond, she saw her mother and Earl turning toward the commotion, their expressions shifting from surprise to concern as they realized what was happening.

Her mother's eyes locked with Capri's across the aisle, and in that moment, Capri saw the pain, the understanding, and something more—something that filled her with shame. She wasn't just caught by Nicola; she was caught by the very woman she had been so desperate to protect.

Earl let go of her mother's hand, stepping back slightly as if giving them space, but the damage was done. The air between them all felt thick with unspoken words and tension.

Capri opened her mouth to say something, anything, but the words wouldn't come.

Nicola's eyes glittered with cruel satisfaction, waiting for the drama to unfold.

Capri's mother, though, was the first to speak, her voice steady but soft. "Capri, honey, we need to talk." There was no anger in her tone, just a quiet plea that broke something in Capri's resolve.

She nodded numbly, her eyes darting away from Nicola's victorious gaze, and followed her mother and Earl toward the back of the store, where the aisles were quieter, and they could have some semblance of privacy.

As they moved away, Capri could still feel the weight of Nicola's stare, could hear the murmurs of curiosity from other shoppers who had overheard the exchange. Her mother didn't say anything until they reached the end of the aisle, where the store opened up into a small seating area with a coffee machine and a few old magazines.

She turned to face Capri, her expression gentle but firm. "I know this is hard for you," she began, her eyes searching Capri's for some sign of understanding. "But Earl... he's been a good friend to me. And I never wanted you to feel like this, but honey...we're in love."

Capri wanted to argue. Love? She was a widow of less than a couple of months. No one falls in love this quickly.

She wanted to tell her mother how wrong this all felt, but she couldn't deny the warmth in her mother's eyes, the way Earl stood by her side, not pushing, just waiting.

Capri stood there, trying to swallow the lump building in her throat.

For the first time, Capri realized that maybe, just maybe, her mother had found something worth holding on to, even if it wasn't what Capri wanted to see. The thought left her feeling more lost than ever but also strangely relieved, like maybe she didn't have to carry all the weight of the past alone.

Capri swallowed hard, her heart pounding as she struggled to process the scene before her. Her mother's face was filled with indescribable happiness—a joy Capri couldn't understand, much less accept.

Earl placed a protective arm around her mom's shoulder. His normally unruly hair was slicked down with product. He'd exchanged his normal overalls for jeans and a button-down shirt. He exchanged glances with her mother. She nodded, and he cleared his throat.

"I've asked your mother to marry me."

Capri felt the ground sway beneath her, the words hitting her like a punch to the gut. Her breath caught in her throat as she stared at Earl, the image of him standing there, so polished and out of character, only adding to the surrealness of the moment. His arm around her mother's shoulders, his hair slicked down, the unfamiliar clothes—everything about him seemed wrong, like a stranger had taken his place. But it wasn't just the change in his appearance; it was the certainty in his voice, the way he looked at her mother with an affection that was undeniable.

Capri's chest tightened, her heart pounding in her ears as she struggled to find her voice, to process the shock that rippled through her. But all she could do was stand there, frozen, her mind racing with the implications of his words and the overwhelming realization that nothing—not even the memories of her life with Dick—would ever feel secure or unchanging again.

"Marry you?" she shrieked, not bothering to lower her voice. "That's ridiculous!" She looked to her mom for confirmation. Surely, she hadn't just learned her mother planned to remarry—while in the grocery store, no less.

Her mother's voice cut through the haze, calm and reassuring, but it did little to ease the ache building in Capri's chest. "I wish we could've talked about this sooner," she said softly, glancing at Earl, who nodded, his expression kind but unreadable. "I wanted to tell you, Capri, but... I didn't know how."

Capri clenched her jaw, trying to keep the emotions in check, but the words tumbled out before she could stop them. "How could you move on so fast?" Her voice cracked, betraying the vulnerability she'd been trying so hard to hide. "It hasn't even been that long, Mom. How can you... how can you do this?"

Her mother's eyes filled with a sadness that mirrored Capri's own. "I'm not trying to replace Dick. I could never do that," she said, her voice barely above a whisper. "But I'm still here, Capri. I'm still alive. And I need to find a way to keep living, even if it means finding comfort in someone else."

Capri looked away, her vision blurring as she tried to hold back tears.

Earl remained silent, his presence a reminder of everything Capri didn't want to confront. She wanted to lash out, to make her mother understand the depth of her hurt, but the words wouldn't come. Instead, she just stood there, feeling the weight of loss and change pressing down on her, suffocating in its inevitability.

Finally, her mother reached out, her touch gentle on Capri's arm. "We'll talk more, okay? I don't want this to be how we leave this conversation. But I need you to know that I care about him, and he cares about me. It's different, but it doesn't mean I've forgotten Dick." She looked to Earl. "Neither of us wants to be alone."

Capri nodded slowly, the fight draining out of her. She couldn't argue with the truth in her mother's words, even if it hurt. "I just... I just need some time," she whispered, her voice thick with emotion.

Her mother smiled faintly, understanding. "Take all the time you need, sweetheart."

As Capri turned to leave, her mind still reeling, she couldn't help but glance back one last time. Her mother and Earl stood there, not quite touching but connected in a way Capri was beginning to realize she'd have to accept. She walked out of the grocery store, past a gawking Nicola Cavendish; the snide look on her face like alcohol tossed on an open wound.

Outside, the warm June air hit her face, a stark contrast to the chill she felt inside.

Capri stood on the curb, staring out at the quiet town of Thunder Mountain; the familiar streets suddenly feeling foreign. Life was moving on around her, whether she was ready for it or not.

As she walked back to her truck, the realization settled in her bones—nothing would ever be the same again.

9

"Oh, my goodness! You're kidding, right?" Charlie Grace stopped mid-step. "What do you mean Capri's mom plans to remarry?"

Lila nodded. "It's all over town, thanks to Nicola Cavendish. She was there in the Western Drug and General when it happened." She reached for a pretzel from the bowl on Charlie Grace's coffee table.

Reva held up both her hands. "Wait, back up. Are you telling me Capri learned of this while in the grocery store?"

Lila shrugged. "That's what I heard."

Charlie Grace placed the tray with the martini glasses on the coffee table beside the bowl. She picked up the lone tumbler filled with ice and soda and handed it to Reva. "Oh, that's awful."

Reva scowled as she took the glass. "We shouldn't be shocked. Before Dick entered the picture, Emily Jacobs had quite the dating history. Remember when we were in grade school? Capri would go home to a new man almost every week."

Lila nodded. "I do. Some of them even came from as far as Cheyenne. There always seemed to be a flock of buzzards circling if I remember right."

Reva looked across the sofa at her friends. "Emily is the type of woman who always needs a partner to feel complete, convinced that her worth is tied to being someone's significant other." Her jaw stiffened. "Even when that need tramples the needs of your daughter." She shook her head. "Announcing your engagement in the grocery store. Who does that?"

"Oh, I feel so bad for Capri. This must be a shock." Lila glanced between the others. "And Earl Dunlop? The guy who brings his kitten into the vet's office? He's the town bachelor, well...one of many."

A tiny grin sprouted on Reva's lips. "At least Emily isn't dating someone with a pit bull or a Doberman. That says something, I guess."

Charlie Grace nodded. "Yeah, Dick was a real junkyard dog before he finally got sober."

The sound of an approaching vehicle drew their attention.

Reva set her glass down. "Looks like our friend's here."

Capri's red truck rolled into the yard, the engine cutting off as she parked. They watched as she hopped out, sprinting to the door and taking the porch steps two at a time. She knocked twice then pushed the door open.

"Hey, guys!" Her eyes were bright, and she was smiling.

The others looked at each other, puzzled.

"Glad you made it, Capri," Charlie Grace said, walking over and giving her a shoulder hug. She led her friend over to the sofa and placed a martini glass filled with blue liquid into her hand. "These are called Seven Seas Martinis. I got the recipe on Pinterest. They're made with Blue Curacao liqueur."

Capri took a sip. "Delicious." She looked around. Where's your dad and Jewel?"

Still looking puzzled, Charlie Grace grabbed a pretzel and sat down on the sofa beside Lila. "They're over at Aunt Mo's playing cards with Nick. He's making a real effort to connect and spend time with my dad. I can't tell you what that's done for Dad's temperament. I think he's been lonely."

Capri knocked back the martini glass and drained the liquid. She set the glass down with a tight smile. "Well, I hear there's an easy remedy for that loneliness thing. He could follow in my mom's footsteps and get back out there, start dating. Nothing says 'I'm desperate' like two old folks trying to pretend they're not past their prime."

Reva rested her elbows on her knees and looked her friend square in the eyes. "Honey, we heard."

Capri threw her head back, laughing. "Oh, don't get me wrong. I'm happy for them. Apparently, Mom has found love again for the twelfth time. Crazy me, I thought she might be done after Dick. But nope. She's getting married again." She grabbed her empty glass and thrust it in Charlie Grace's direction. "Could I have another Pinterest drink, please?"

She turned to the others. "Actually, she's eloping. At least that's what she said last night. That could change. Goodness knows, Mom is filled with surprises these days."

Charlie Grace reached over and squeezed Capri's arm. "It must be hard seeing your mom move on, but maybe this is her way of finding some happiness again. It doesn't mean she's forgotten your stepdad or what you two shared."

Reva nodded in agreement. "Yeah, sometimes people need to feel like they're still living, even after a loss. It doesn't take away from what they had before."

Capri let out a short, bitter laugh. "Oh, I'm sure she's feeling alive, alright. I just hope she doesn't break a hip in the process. But hey, who am I to judge? Maybe the secret to eternal youth is pretending the last fifty years didn't happen."

She looked to Charlie Grace. "And about that drink..."

Charlie Grace reluctantly moved for the kitchen and refilled her friend's glass with the martini mixture. She carried it carefully into the living room and placed it in Capri's hand. "I think Earl Dunlop is a nice man. That's good, right?"

Capri shrugged. "Well, at least he's got money. Will relieve me and my bank accounts of the financial burden."

Reva's eyebrows raised with shock. "He's got money?"

Capri took a long sip from her martini. "Yup. They plan to elope and then get this...he's moving my mother to some property he owns in Idaho. They are going to live in a fifth wheel while he builds her the house of her dreams. Anything she wants, she gets." Despite her stiff body language, her eyes shone with unshed tears. "I guess she finally found her prince."

She shrugged it all off. "But, who cares, right? Life moves on." She emptied the glass a second time, then wiped her mouth with the back of her hand before slamming the stemmed glassware onto the table. Thankfully, it didn't break.

Lila's brow furrowed with concern. "Capri, you don't have to pretend this doesn't bother you. We're here for you, no matter what."

Capri shrugged, her voice laced with sarcasm. "What's there to be bothered about? My mom's living her best life, right? And I get to sit front row for the show. It's like watching a slow-motion train wreck with a side of prune juice. Real riveting stuff."

Reva watched as what little color Capri had drained from her face. Her expression held a resigned and profound despair.

Capri's relationship with her mother had always been a tangled mess of duty and resentment. From a young age, Capri had stepped into the role of caretaker, managing her mother's moods and insecurities, finding her own sense of purpose in keeping things together. Her mother's fragile dependence gave Capri a reason to stay strong, to be the rock in the storm. But now, as her mother sought comfort in someone else, Capri no doubt felt unmoored, her sense of purpose slipping away, leaving her with a bitterness she couldn't quite mask.

Couple that with Dick's passing and there was no mistaking that their dear friend was going to need their support—now more than ever.

10

In typical fashion, Capri's mom thought food could fix everything. Despite the stacked boxes and luggage at the door waiting to be loaded into Earl's U-Haul, Capri was forced to sit at the table and eat, acting as though the bottom wasn't falling out from under her.

"Honey, is that all you want?" her mother posed. "I fixed your favorite. You love spaghetti and meatballs." She turned to Earl, who had cleaned his plate so efficiently by scraping a piece of bread across the surface and then eating the last remaining sauce. "Would you like seconds, darling?"

"You mean thirds," Capri muttered.

"What, honey?"

Capri drew a deep breath and shoved aside her plate. "Nothing. Not important." Okay, yes—she might be acting like a spoiled little girl but the child inside of her was screaming.

She looked across the table to Earl, who was oblivious to her pain. He had a tiny bit of sauce clinging to his mustache. Seeing it, her mom picked up a napkin and lovingly tapped at the side of his mouth, cleaning the spot.

"Thanks, Princess."

Oh, my goodness! *Kill her now!*

If Earl Dunlop called her mother Princess one more time, she was going to vomit spaghetti all over the table.

Her mother stood and cleared the table. Normally, Capri would hurry her back to her seat, offering to take over the task. Today, she sat, her arms folded across her chest, and sullenly stared straight at the door with the stacked boxes.

"I made a chocolate ganache cake." Her mother made a big production of slicing the dessert and carried over small plates laden with the sweet confection. "Here you go, baby." She set a plate in front of Earl. In response, he playfully patted her bottom as she turned to get another helping from the counter.

Her mother giggled like a silly schoolgirl.

As soon as her mom set the slice before her, along with a fork, Capri simply slid the plate aside. "No thanks."

Her mom and Earl exchanged glances but said nothing in response to her spoiled brat act.

Truly, she did not want to be this way. She should be happy for her mother and her upcoming nuptials. Shouldn't she?

Instead, her gut felt like it was filled with river rock.

A short while later, her mother picked up the remaining lunch dishes and loaded the dishwasher. She wiped down the counter and carefully folded the washcloth and placed it next to the sink. She turned. "Well, I guess I'm done."

Capri wondered at the double meaning of the phrase. Done with the dishes? Or, done with the life she had here with Capri?

Earl's face filled with giddy anticipation. "We'll call as soon as we get to Vegas," he told her. Their plans were to make the five-hour drive as far as Salt Lake City, spend the night, then proceed into Sin City in the morning. They'd stay at the Stratosphere Hotel and Casino, then head to the infamous Little White Chapel for a ten o'clock ceremony.

"Honey, did you know Joan Collins and Michael Jordan

both had their wedding ceremonies at the Little White Chapel?" her mother said, excitement lacing her words.

Her mother moved for the door. "Do you need help, honey?"

"Nah, I got this," Earl assured her.

As Earl carried the boxes outside and into the U-Haul, her mother turned to her. "I'll send pictures."

Capri nodded absent-mindedly. "Yeah, sure. That'd be nice."

When Earl picked up the last of the suitcases, he grunted. "Goodness, Emily. What do you have in here?"

She smiled. "Just a few keepsakes," she told him. Her new diamond engagement ring sparkled as it caught the sunlight as they followed Earl onto the porch.

Her mom suddenly turned; her eyes filled with tears. "I love you, baby." She pulled Capri into a tight hug, gripping her like a vise. When she finally let go, she brushed a kiss against Capri's cheek and then ran for Earl's vehicle, too filled with emotion to turn back.

In the distance, black thunderclouds rumbled in over the tops of the mountain peaks, leaving the air heavy. It was as if the sky was turning edgy, tense, and expectant, waiting for the inevitable storm to hit.

Earl stood still on the porch, looking uncomfortable. "I'll take good care of her," he promised, his voice strong and earnest.

Capri felt her throat closing with emotion. She simply nodded and looked at this man, staring at the buttons on his shirt, as if that would provide a clue as to why her mother loved him.

Then he leaned forward, looking her in the eyes, and a weird thing happened—he drew her into an awkward embrace.

She was unsure whether or not she could hug him back. With all the effort she could muster, she lifted her arms and placed them on the other side of his robust frame. Clearing her throat, she gave him a slight hug.

When he stepped back from her, he paused, softening, but pressing on. "I love her, you know." There was an intensity in the man's eyes—the kind that signaled Earl thought he was the luckiest man on the earth. His expression was raw and vulnerable yet filled with strength.

"Some people would say that's a good thing," he added. Then, he turned and joined her mother in the car.

Capri watched as her mother waved wildly from inside the truck. She kissed the palm of her hand and threw the kiss in her direction, just like when Capri was a little girl.

Earl started the engine. Capri released a long sigh as he pulled slowly out, circled the drive, and proceeded down the lane toward the highway.

And just like that, she was alone.

11

C apri Jacobs tugged the brim of her baseball cap lower, blocking out the glare of the late afternoon sun. Her hands were steady, calloused fingers deftly working on the engine of Dick's old truck parked outside her cabin. It was the same truck he'd taught her to tinker with when she was just a kid, the one they'd spent countless hours fixing together. She could practically hear his voice, guiding her, telling her to "keep at it until it purrs like a kitten."

Today, though, the truck's stubborn silence mirrored the turmoil inside her. Her mother's sudden marriage to Earl had left Capri feeling untethered, like a raft with no anchor. The small cabin that once bustled with laughter, arguments, and shared meals now echoed with emptiness.

Fixing things—engines, appliances, even the old wooden steps leading up to the porch—was something Capri had always done. But now, it had become her lifeline, a way to keep her hands busy and her mind from spiraling into the abyss of loneliness that seemed to grow wider each day.

She had no one to blame but herself. No one had made her devote her life to taking care of her mom and Dick—making sure the bills were paid, the doctor appointments were scheduled, and their lives were kept whole and happy. She'd even paid off the house to keep them debt-free.

But now here she was.

She straightened up, wiping her hands on a rag, and stared out at the distant mountains. The peaks, still dusted with snow even in the early months of summer, had always been her refuge. But today, they offered no comfort. With a sigh, she reached for her phone, a desperate thought flickering through her mind.

Charlie Grace would know how to make her feel better. Her friend had a way of seeing the world through a different lens—literally since she was always behind one these days. Capri dialed her number, hoping to hear a familiar voice.

"Hey, Capri!" Her girlfriend's voice came through the cell phone, bright and cheerful as always.

"Hey," Capri replied, trying to match her friend's energy. "I was thinking maybe we could grab coffee or something? I'd love to catch up, just you and me."

There was a pause, and Capri could almost see Charlie's face, her lips pursed in thought. "I'd love to, but I'm swamped with this photography exhibit in Jackson Hole. It's opening in a few days, and I've got to get everything just right. Rain check?"

Capri forced a smile, though the rejection stung. "Yeah, sure. No problem. Good luck with the exhibit."

After hanging up, Capri tried Reva. If anyone could spare a moment, it would be her. Reva was always the quintessential friend, the one who had a knack for making everyone feel at home. Maybe they could meet for lunch.

"Capri, hi!" Reva's voice was warm, but there was an undercurrent of stress. "What's up?"

"I was wondering if you wanted to hang out, maybe grab lunch or something," Capri asked, her voice hopeful.

"Oh, I wish I could. But Lucan's got the sniffles, and I'm

taking him to the doctor just to be safe. You know how I worry," Reva said, a touch of apology in her tone. "Another time? But I'll see you Friday night at Lila's?"

"Of course," Capri said, her heart sinking further. "Give Lucan a hug from me."

Last, she tried Lila. The two of them had always been close, especially since Dick passed. Lila understood what it was like to lose someone, to feel that gaping hole where love used to be.

But Lila was distracted when she answered. "Hey Capri, can I call you back? The clinic's been crazy busy since Doc Tillman left, and Whit and I are trying to keep up. We have six dogs, two cats, and a rabbit in the waiting room. It's been nonstop."

Capri swallowed her disappointment. "Sure, no problem. Good luck with everything."

She didn't bother calling anyone else. She momentarily considered reaching out to the Knit Wit ladies, then the notion dawned that Oma, Betty, and Dorothy would likely be busy with their own lives—grandkids, church dinners, whatever else filled their days.

Oh well, she'd just have to make do with her own company.

Capri shoved her phone into her pocket and glanced at the cabin, her childhood home, the place that held so many memories of her mother and Dick. The kitchen walls were still covered in the same wallpaper her mother had chosen years ago. The creaky floorboards still groaned in the same spots, a familiar soundtrack to a life that was no longer hers. The sofa, the television...the bathroom rugs. Nothing had been updated in years.

The truck's engine remained silent as Capri returned to the porch, where her tools were scattered. She picked up a wrench and gathered the rest of her tools and headed inside the house and straight for the kitchen.

She pulled open the cabinet doors under the sink. The drain had been slow for months.

Capri crouched and positioned herself nearly inside the cabinet, the smell of cleanser filling her nostrils. Her jaw clenched as she attacked the faucet drain with a wrench, her movements quick and forceful. The metal groaned in protest, but she didn't care—she was determined to get it apart. Water dripped steadily from the pipe as she unscrewed the trap, her fingers moving with practiced precision despite the frustration bubbling inside her.

When she finally pried it free, a mass of hair and gunk greeted her, tangled in the curve of the pipe. She yanked it out with a grimace, the mess clinging stubbornly to her fingers.

With a quick rinse, she watched as the water flowed freely again, a small victory in an otherwise uncontrollable world. Capri reassembled the drain with fierce satisfaction, tightening each connection as if she could tighten the loose ends of her life just as easily.

Finally, she stepped back, breathing hard, her hands shaking slightly. The clog was gone, the sink was fixed, but the turmoil inside her was still very much there. Fixing things was what she did best, but no amount of effort could fix the emptiness she felt.

Something inside her snapped, or maybe it was finally piecing itself together. She didn't know. But as she stood there, hands still clutching the wrench, Capri made a decision—a big one. She wasn't ready to say it out loud, not even to herself, but she felt it settle deep within her, solid and unmovable.

Capri dropped the wrench, the metal clanging loudly against the wooden floor, echoing in the empty cabin. She turned and walked outside, leaving the door ajar, the decision she had made growing stronger with every step.

Outside, Capri turned and surveyed the cabin, her eyes tracing the familiar lines of the weathered wood, the chipped paint on the window frames, and the sagging porch that she and Dick had promised to fix "someday."

The small structure stood nestled against the backdrop of towering pines, almost swallowed by the vastness of the mountains beyond. It looked as tired as she felt, worn down by years of holding everything together. The once-cozy home now seemed like a relic of another life—a life filled with laughter, shared meals, and late-night conversations by the fire. But now, it felt hollow, a shell of what it used to be, mirroring the emptiness inside her.

The memories were everywhere—the spot where she and her mother had planted flowers that now struggled to bloom because Capri had likely overwatered them. The swing on the porch where she and Dick would sit in silence, both knowing that words weren't always necessary. Capri's gaze lingered on the front door, its paint faded from years of exposure to the elements.

This was the place where she had learned the value of hard work, of loyalty, of love. But now, it was also the place where she felt abandoned, left to pick up the pieces of a life that no longer made sense.

She took a deep breath, the cool mountain air filling her lungs, and felt a bittersweet pang in her chest. This cabin had been her sanctuary, her refuge from the world. But now, it was just another thing that needed fixing—only this time, no amount of effort could restore what had been lost.

As she looked at the cabin, she realized that it was time to let go, to stop trying to mend what was beyond repair. The unlikely decision she had made felt like both a burden and a relief, heavy with the weight of finality yet light with the promise of something new.

With one last look, Capri turned away, knowing that whatever came next, it wouldn't be within these walls. She was ready to move forward, even if it meant leaving a part of herself behind.

12

Reva sat at their usual corner table in the Rustic Pine, the warm, wood-paneled walls and dim lighting creating a cozy, familiar atmosphere. She glanced around the room, her gaze settling on the door just as Lila and Charlie Grace walked in, both looking a little weary. Lila dropped her bag onto the chair with a sigh, a tired but grateful smile on her face.

"Thanks for being flexible with the meetup," Lila said, her voice tinged with exhaustion. "My place is a disaster zone right now, especially with Camille back from college. Dorm life hasn't exactly cured her of her messy habits."

Charlie Grace gave a knowing laugh, shaking her head as she slid into her seat. "No judgment from me. Believe me, I get it. The guest ranch is packed to the brim now that tourist season is in full swing. I'm juggling a full house with reservations lined up for weeks."

Reva and Lila exchanged impressed looks, and Reva nodded. "That's wonderful, Charlie Grace. You've worked so hard for this."

Charlie Grace smiled, a mix of pride and exhaustion in her

eyes. "It makes me happy, but it's tough juggling everything. Raising Jewel, managing the ranch, and getting ready for the big photography exhibit in Jackson Hole...it's a lot."

Lila took out her wallet. "Tell us more about the exhibit. How's everything coming along?"

Charlie Grace's face lit up as she launched into the details, sharing her excitement about the exhibit. "Nick has been amazing, helping me prepare. I'm nervous, but more than that, I'm excited. It's a huge opportunity."

Reva grinned, noticing the subtle shift in Charlie Grace's expression. "Speaking of Nick," she teased. "How are things going with him?"

Charlie Grace slid her credit card in Lila's direction before answering. "And, about Nick." She paused, a sly smile forming. "All I can say is that falling for that hunk was like finding the perfect pair of boots—unexpected, but now I can't imagine my life without them."

Lila chuckled and pushed the credit card back. "I've got this."

Reva's mind drifted to Capri. She glanced at the door, frowning slightly. "Capri's late...again."

The mood shifted slightly, and the women shared a look of concern. Lila sighed. "She did reach out, but I couldn't get away from the clinic."

Charlie Grace nodded. "Same here. I wanted to be there for her, but it's been so hectic."

Reva folded her hands, her voice firm but gentle. "We all need to step up and be better friends. Capri's going through a lot right now."

Just as the weight of the conversation settled, the door to the Rustic Pine burst open, drawing their attention. Capri strode in, a confident smile on her face, but what shocked them all was the unknown cowboy with his arm around her.

He pulled her close, planting a kiss on her lips in front of everyone before tipping his hat and heading back out the door with a promise to see her again soon.

Capri sauntered over to the table, slid into the seat next to Reva, who exchanged stunned glances with the others, struggling to reconcile this version of Capri with the friend they knew. Capri was not someone who casually hooked up with men. Yet, she'd been seen with several guys lately.

"Who was that?" Lila asked, her tone laced with disbelief.

Capri shrugged, her smile still in place. "Just someone I met. He's visiting from Cheyenne. But not to worry, I won't be seeing him again. He's too boring."

The table fell into an uneasy silence. Reva was the first to find her voice. "Capri...are you okay?"

Capri dismissed her concern with a wave of her hand. "I'm fine. Never better."

But Reva wasn't convinced, and neither were the others. They knew Capri, and this wasn't like her at all.

Unspoken concern lingered in the air as Reva tried to understand what their friend was going through and how they could help her navigate this storm.

Before Reva or the others could prod for more information, Capri's expression lit up. "Oh, I have news."

"News?" Annie asked as she neared the table to take their order.

Capri turned to her. "Yeah. Great news actually."

Reva and the others leaned forward. "Tell us," Reva urged.

Capri took a deep breath, her eyes sparkling with a mix of excitement and resolve. "I've decided to tear down my mom's house and rebuild it from the ground up." She knotted her ponytail at the nape of her neck. "Before Mom left with Earl, she reminded me she deeded the house over to me back when I turned eighteen—when Dick was drinking, and she was afraid he'd do something to put them in financial jeopardy. She has no plans to return to Thunder Mountain and told me the property is now mine. I can do what I want with it." She leaned her elbows on the table. "And I plan to tear the house down."

A brief silence followed as her friends processed the weight of her announcement. Reva exchanged a quick glance with Lila and Charlie Grace, trying to gauge their reactions to see if they were as stunned by this news as she was.

"Wow," Lila finally said, her voice cautious. "That's a big decision, Capri."

"It is," Capri nodded, her tone firm. "But it feels right. That little cabin—it holds so many memories, but it's also a reminder of everything that's changed. I think it's time to start fresh, you know?"

Charlie Grace leaned back in her chair, studying Capri with a mix of admiration and concern. "Are you sure you're ready for that? Rebuilding is a huge project, emotionally and financially."

Capri shrugged, a determined smile on her lips. "Money's no object. Besides, I've thought about it long and hard. This isn't just about the house—it's about me, too. It's time I fix what's been broken and create something new, something that's mine."

Reva, sensing the deeper meaning behind Capri's words, reached across the table to squeeze her hand. "If anyone can pull this off, it's you. Just remember, you don't have to do it alone."

Capri's expression softened, the bravado giving way to vulnerability. "Thanks, Reva. I might need a few hands along the way."

Annie, who had been quietly listening, broke the tension with a bright smile. "Well, that sounds like a reason to celebrate. How about some drinks on the house?"

The offer brought a round of laughter, easing the seriousness of the moment. As Annie took their orders and headed back to the bar, the friends returned their focus to Capri.

"So," Charlie Grace said, her tone lightening. "Do you have a plan in mind, or are you just going to swing a hammer and see what happens?"

Capri laughed, the sound genuine and warm. "I've got some ideas. But first, I need to get the old place down. That's going to be cathartic, I think."

Lila smiled, the tension in her posture easing. "We'll be there to cheer you on—or swing a hammer if you need."

"Absolutely," Reva agreed, nodding firmly. "Whatever you need, we're here."

Capri's eyes shimmered with gratitude as she looked around the table at her friends. "I'm lucky to have you all. Really. But I will have to hire a contractor, no doubt. I've already started researching options."

Annie returned to the table and passed out their drinks.

Charlie Grace lifted her mug of beer. "Here's to Capri...and her rebuild."

They all raised their glasses and joined the toast, laughing just like old times.

Reva leaned back, a satisfied smile on her face as the conversation shifted to lighter topics. But in the back of her mind, she knew Capri's decision was about more than just a house. It was about reclaiming her life.

Reva was determined to support her every step of the way.

13

Capri woke to the sound of a car engine outside. She threw back the covers and jumped from her bed, completely dressed...and a little confused as to why. The nearly empty tequila bottle on the bedside table might be her first clue.

Alarmed, she glanced back at the bed. Thankfully, the spot beside where she'd slept was empty and from the looks of the bedcovers, had been that way all night. She rubbed her temples as the pain in her head pounded, promising to lay off the sauce.

The engine rumbled to a stop. Curiosity got the better of her, and she risked a glance out the window, only to let out a groan.

With a determined sigh, she raced for the bathroom, splashed some water on her face, and rinsed out her mouth, cupping the water in her hands for lack of a proper glass. She straightened her hair with her fingers and pulled it back into a ponytail, then fastened the strands with a rubber band as she raced for the front door.

As soon as she pulled it open and stepped onto the porch,

Capri's eyes landed on a guy climbing out of a pickup truck. Despite her throbbing head, her heart did a double take.

The guy was ruggedly handsome, with a strong build that spoke of hard work, his tanned skin a testament to hours spent under the sun. As he walked around and opened the back passenger door on his truck, reaching for a leatherbound note-book, he did so with subdued focus. His tousled brown hair and the hint of stubble on his jawline added to his laid-back demeanor.

"Hey, you're early," she called out, not bothering with a more inviting greeting.

He glanced at his watch and shook his head. "Nope. Right on time."

She decided to give him that one, knowing that was entirely possible given her late start. "Well, don't just stand there. Come in and take a look around."

She waited for him to climb the steps to the porch before she granted him the slightest of smiles.

His eyes caught her off guard—blue, sharp, and filled with a quiet determination. There was a stubbornness in his gaze, a pride that seemed to come from knowing exactly who he was and where he came from.

She was a good judge of character, and this one exuded an air of independence, a man who was unapologetically himself, with a quiet confidence that seemed to say he wasn't easily rattled. There was no pretense, just a calm assurance that dared her to match his unflinching steadiness with her own.

Despite her wrinkled blouse and no make-up, she was up for the challenge.

"You got a name?" she demanded.

He let a slow smile tug at the corner of his mouth as if amused by her directness. "Same as when we talked on the phone. Jake Carrington," he said, tipping his baseball cap slightly in a casual gesture of respect. "I'm the contractor you called about the renovation work." His voice was smooth, with a hint of an unmistakable Southern drawl. He extended a hand toward her, calloused but steady, waiting for her to make the next move. "I'm guessing you're Capri Jacobs."

Capri hesitated for just a beat, her gaze flicking from his hand to his eyes, searching for any hint of condescension. Finding none, she accepted the handshake, his grip firm but not overbearing. "That's right," she confirmed, pulling her hand back a little too quickly. She crossed her arms over her chest, a habit she'd picked up whenever she felt the need to shield herself.

"So, you think you're up for this?" she asked, tilting her chin up slightly, challenging him again. It wasn't just the rebuild she was asking about—it was perhaps a little more, though she wasn't sure she'd admit that, even to herself.

Jake's smile didn't waver. If anything, it deepened as if he could read the unspoken layers of her question. "I've handled worse," he said with an easy shrug. "But why don't you show me around, and I'll let you know for sure." His tone was professional, yet there was an underlying attitude that suggested he wasn't just here for a paycheck—he genuinely cared about doing the job right.

Capri nodded, her defenses going up. There was something disarming about Jake. It wasn't just his words, but the way he carried himself—calm, unhurried as if he had all the time in the world to listen to her concerns. She wasn't used to that.

People usually came into her life with expectations, demands, or with their own agenda. But Jake seemed different, and that unsettled her in a way she hadn't anticipated. "Alright then, follow me," she said, turning on her heel and leading him back out into the yard where they could get a good view of the exterior.

Jake fell into step beside her without a word.

She gestured at the house with a sweeping motion, her tone matter-of-fact. "I'm thinking we tear it down and start fresh. The place is old, and honestly, it'd be easier to just rebuild." Then, to emphasize her point, "Money is no object." She walked to the side of the house so he could get a full view of what they were dealing with.

Jake stopped in his tracks, his eyes narrowing as he took in the structure. He didn't follow her immediately. Instead, he stepped back to get a better look at the house. His gaze roamed over the weathered wood, the sagging porch, and the chipped paint, but there was no disdain in his expression. Instead, there was a kind of reverence, like he was seeing something she wasn't.

"Hold on a minute," Jake finally said, his voice steady but firm. "Tear it down? That's a bold move, but I'm not sure it's the right one." He walked up to the porch, running a hand along one of the support beams. "This place has good bones, ma'am. Sure, it's seen better days, but there's a lot worth saving here."

Capri crossed her arms again, her skepticism clear. "First of all, drop the ma'am. It's Capri." She followed his gaze. "You see something I don't?" she challenged, tilting her head slightly.

Jake turned to face her, nodding. "Yeah, I do. Look at these joists—they're solid. They don't make them like this anymore. And the foundation, from what I can tell, is still strong. This house has character, history. You tear it down, and you lose all that. It's not just about convenience; it's about preserving what's here, what's real."

He took a step closer to her, his voice softening. "I get it. You want something new and shiny. But sometimes the best way to move forward is to work with what you've got. Fix what's broken, restore what's worn, and keep the soul of the place intact."

Capri felt a flicker of something—was it doubt? Or was it the beginning of conviction? She glanced back at the house, trying to see it through his eyes. The peeling paint and creaking boards no longer seemed like obstacles but challenges; ones that could be met with the right kind of care. She turned back to Jake, her defenses lowering just a fraction.

"You really think it's worth it?" she asked, her voice quieter now, less certain.

Jake met her gaze, his expression earnest. "I wouldn't say it if I didn't. This house has a story, and I think it's one worth continuing."

She felt a subtle warmth rise in her chest, one she quickly tried to push aside, telling herself it was just the summer heat.

"Fine," she said, her voice carrying the same firmness she always used to mask uncertainty. "We'll do this your way." The words tasted foreign on her tongue—she wasn't used to conceding, especially not to someone she barely knew. But there was something about Jake Carrington that made her feel like maybe, just this once, letting someone else take the lead might not be the worst idea.

A small smile tugged at the corner of Jake's mouth, but he didn't gloat. Instead, he gave a single nod as if acknowledging the weight of her decision. "You won't regret it," he said simply.

Capri nodded, though she wasn't entirely sure she believed him. "Let's hope not," she replied, trying to regain some of her usual edge. She turned toward the house again, taking in its weathered facade with a fresh perspective. "So, what's the next step?"

Jake stepped onto the porch beside her, the boards creaking under his weight. "I'll put together a detailed plan. We'll need to assess the full structure, get a list of what needs replacing and what can be restored. It's going to take time and patience, but if we do it right, this place will be something special."

She listened, catching the undercurrent of passion in his voice. He wasn't just talking about a construction project that would make him money; this was about creating something meaningful. The subtle attraction she felt earlier simmered quietly in the background, but she shoved it aside, focusing on the task ahead.

"Alright," she said, more to herself than to him. "Let's get started."

They spent the next hour walking through the house, Jake pointing out details she had overlooked—exposed brick behind the drywall, original wood floors beneath the carpet. He spoke with a reverence for the craftsmanship that had gone into building the home, and Capri found herself drawn to his knowledge, his respect for the past.

They walked through every room, discussing possibilities, and mapping out a vision for the house's future. By the time they wrapped up, Capri found herself unexpectedly absorbed in the project, his passion for the work subtly infectious.

As they finished, Capri stood in the doorway, watching as Jake packed up his pen and notebook, his movements efficient and sure. She realized she was watching him a little too closely and quickly looked away, feeling a strange mix of anticipation and unease settle in her chest.

"We'll meet again next week," Jake said, slinging his bag over his shoulder. "I'll have the plan ready by then."

"Next week," Capri repeated, more to ground herself than anything else. She needed time to process, to figure out why she was so unsettled by this man.

Jake gave her one last nod before heading to his truck. As he drove away, the rumble of the engine fading into the distance, Capri stood on the porch. The house loomed behind her, a silent witness to the change she'd just set in motion. She wasn't sure where this project would take her, but for the first time in a long while, she felt something other than the weight of loss.

Capri turned back toward the house, her mind swirling with thoughts she wasn't ready to unpack. Not yet. But as she walked inside, closing the door behind her, she couldn't shake the feeling that maybe, just maybe, she was on the brink of something new.

14

Reva stood at the edge of the Moose Chapel grounds, taking in the scene as the final touches were added to the vacation bible school setup. The centerpiece of it all was the massive wooden ark, its beams solid and strong, thanks to the direction of Charlie Grace's father, Clancy Rivers. The old man sat in his wheelchair nearby, a satisfied smile on his face as he watched a few ranch hands finish up the last of the decorations—Charlie Grace's ex-husband, Gibbs Nichols, among them.

The ark itself was a sight to behold, stretching nearly the length of the chapel, with hand-painted animals peeking out from every window. Colorful streamers in blue, green, and gold fluttered in the breeze, mimicking the flow of water, while pairs of stuffed animals were scattered across the ground, ready to be collected by eager children.

The scene was set against a backdrop of the majestic Teton mountain peaks and a landscape filled with pastel-colored lupines and dotted with sagebrush. The breeze caught the aspen leaves, making them shimmer like silver coins in the sunlight, while the air was rich with the scent of pine and sagebrush. A few hollyhocks sprouting around the church added a touch of deeper color, their tall stalks swaying gently.

Charlie Grace and Lila were busy organizing the craft stations, making sure the paints and brushes were all in place. Capri, on the other hand, hovered near the edge of the gathering, looking a bit out of place. Reva caught her eye and gave her a reassuring smile.

"Capri, you okay?" Reva asked, walking over.

Capri shrugged, her hands tucked into the pockets of her jeans. "This just isn't my thing, you know? I'm not exactly the maternal type."

Reva chuckled. "You don't have to be. Just keep an eye on the kids, make sure they don't get into too much trouble. They'll love you."

Before Capri could respond, Reva's little boy, Lucan, came dashing up, his eyes wide with excitement. "Mommy, Mommy! Did you see the ark? It's HUGE! Can we go inside? Are there real animals?"

Reva crouched down to his level, ruffling his hair. "No real animals, sweetheart, but you can pretend. Isn't that fun?"

Lucan nodded eagerly, then ran off toward the ark, where a group of children had already gathered, pointing and giggling.

"Look, Mom!" one little girl exclaimed, tugging at her mother's hand. "I found a giraffe!"

Her mother laughed. "Yes, there's a pair of giraffes." She pointed. "And a pair of tigers."

Pastor Pete and his wife, Annie, approached the group, their faces beaming with gratitude. "This is more than we could have hoped for," Pastor Pete said, his voice filled with emotion. "You've all outdone yourselves. The kids are going to remember this for a long time."

Annie nodded in agreement, her hands clasped together. "Thank you so much for your hard work, everyone. It means the world to us."

Charlie Grace, wiping her hands on a rag, joined the group. "We're just glad to be a part of it. Clancy here deserves most of the credit, though. That ark is a masterpiece."

Clancy waved off the praise with a modest grin. "Just doing what I can. Couldn't have done it without the help of these fine folks." He nodded toward Gibbs, who gave a brief nod back.

Capri, still lingering on the outskirts, finally stepped forward. "Alright, I guess I'll help wrangle the kids," she said, a hint of reluctance in her voice. "But if any of them try to bite me, I'm out."

Lila laughed. "Don't worry, Capri. If anyone can handle a few wild animals, it's you."

As the children continued to arrive, their faces lit up with excitement, the atmosphere on the Moose Chapel grounds grew even more vibrant. The sound of laughter filled the air, mixing with the aroma of freshly baked cookies as the Knit Wit ladies arrived and began to unpack their contribution to the effort. It was going to be a day to remember, and Reva felt a deep sense of satisfaction knowing she had helped bring it all together.

Reva stood near the refreshment table, passing out cookies and small cartons of milk to the children as they gathered around. The kids were all smiles, their laughter ringing out as they eagerly grabbed their treats.

"Remember, only one cookie each," Reva called out, though she couldn't help but smile when a few of the more mischievous ones tried to sneak a second.

Capri, who had surprisingly taken to her role of wrangling the kids, nudged one little boy with a mock stern look. "That means you too, young man. No doubling up on the chocolate chips."

The boy grinned up at her, crumbs already clinging to his face. "But they're so good, Miss Capri!"

"Nice try," Capri said, her voice softened by a small smile. "Now, go sit down before Pastor Pete starts the story."

The children, still chattering excitedly, found spots on the large blankets spread out in front of the ark. Pastor Pete stood near the front, his Bible in hand, ready to share the tale of Noah's Ark.

"Alright, everyone," Pastor Pete began, his voice warm and inviting. "We're going to talk about a very special story today, one that's all about trusting God to take care of His creation. Do you know what story that is?"

"Noah's Ark!" a chorus of voices shouted back.

"That's right," Pastor Pete said with a smile. He opened the Bible, though the story was clearly already written in his heart. "Noah was a good man—an obedient man—who lived a long time ago. God told him to build a big boat—"

Suddenly, a low rumble interrupted Pastor Pete's words, vibrating through the ground beneath their feet. It started softly, almost like a distant growl, but quickly grew in intensity. The children's chatter quieted as they looked around in confusion.

"Mommy, what's happening?" Lucan's voice was small, filled with uncertainty as he grabbed onto Reva's leg.

Reva's heart skipped a beat, her eyes darting around as the tremor grew stronger. The ground beneath them seemed to ripple, and she instinctively crouched down to hold Lucan close. "It's just a little earthquake, sweetie. Stay close to me."

The tremors intensified, and Reva's gaze snapped to the massive ark, which began to sway precariously on its wooden supports. Shouts of alarm rose as the structure started to tilt.

"Watch out!" Clancy shouted, his voice strong despite the fear in his eyes.

"Everyone, move away from the ark!" Charlie Grace called out, her voice carrying over the growing panic.

Gibbs and the ranch hands sprang into action, trying to

stabilize the ark, but it was too late. With a loud creak, the ark began to topple, its beams groaning under the strain. The children screamed, scrambling to get out of the way.

"Grab the kids!" Reva yelled, her voice nearly drowned out by the chaos. She scooped Lucan into her arms, her heart pounding as she scrambled away from the falling structure. Capri and Lila were already herding the children to safety, their faces tight with concentration.

The ark hit the ground with a thunderous crash, sending a cloud of dust into the air. For a moment, everything was still; the only sound the distant rustling of the aspen leaves in the breeze.

"Is everyone okay?" Pastor Pete's voice cut through the silence, his tone shaky but steady.

Reva scanned the area, her eyes wide. "Is everyone accounted for? Capri? Lila? Charlie Grace?"

"Over here!" Lila called back, holding a little girl close to her chest. "We've got all the kids, I think."

Capri's voice came from the other side, slightly breathless. "I've got four over here. Everyone's okay."

Dorothy clutched Oma's arm. "Wow," she muttered. "That was a strong one."

Charlie Grace scooted closer to where Clancy sat, a look of relief on her face. "Dad? You alright?"

Clancy nodded, though his hands were trembling on the armrests of his wheelchair. "I'm fine, sweetheart. Just... surprised."

Reva clutched Lucan tightly, her heart still racing. "Pastor Pete, that's two earthquakes in as many weeks."

Pastor Pete's face was pale as he looked around, his hands still gripping his Bible. "Yes, and these tremors... they're getting stronger, and longer. That one shook the earth for several seconds."

Annie, her own voice shaky, added, "We need to check on the chapel, make sure everything's still standing."

One of the Knit Wit ladies, Betty Dunning, who was usually the first to dismiss anything unusual, shook her head, her cookies forgotten in her lap. "I've lived here for seventy years, and I've never felt the earth move like this before. Not twice in a row."

Gibbs wiped the sweat from his brow, his eyes scanning the damaged ark. "We'll have to rebuild it, that's for sure. But first, let's get these kids back to their parents. We don't want anyone getting hurt."

As the group slowly began to gather their bearings, the air was thick with tension, each of them glancing at the ground as if expecting it to shake again at any moment.

Lila, looking a bit shaken, helped guide the children away from the wreckage. "This is starting to feel a little unsettling," she muttered, mostly to herself.

Reva reached over and squeezed her hand. "We've handled plenty of earthquakes, Lila. And there will likely be more. There's nothing to get overly anxious about," she said, keeping her voice steady and reassuring.

But, as she looked around at the concerned faces of her friends and neighbors and noted the way her phone was blowing up with text messages, Reva couldn't help but join them in their concern.

The earth, in all its beauty and complexity, usually felt steady beneath their feet, grounding them in their daily lives. But sometimes, it shifted unexpectedly, reminding them that even the most tranquil moments could be disrupted.

While these earthquakes were part of the natural world's rhythms, a reminder of the delicate balance they lived in— when the ground shook, she was no different than the others. She found it unsettling.

As Reva gathered the last of the children, her mind kept

drifting back to the unexpected tremors. They were too frequent, too strong to ignore. She decided right then that she needed answers.

Later, she would reach out to Dr. Grant Marshall, the geologist from the University of Wyoming who had given a talk at the town hall last spring. If anyone could explain why these earthquakes were shaking their normally peaceful town, it would be him.

She had to find out what was going on and, more importantly, what they should be prepared for next.

15

Capri pulled up to Grand Teton Whitewater Adventures. She jumped out of her truck and hurried toward the building, her eyes scanning for any sign of damage.

It didn't take long to find it—a thin crack running along the base of the wall, just under the front window. Capri knelt, running her fingers over the jagged line. It wasn't major, nothing that couldn't be fixed with a bit of mortar and some elbow grease, but her mind still churned with what could have happened. That tremor was strong—and she was hearing about minor damage all over town.

"Capri!" Bodhi's voice called out, pulling her attention away from the crack. He was jogging over from where he'd parked his own truck, his usual laid-back demeanor replaced with a worried frown.

She stood up, brushing the dust off her hands. "Hey, Bodhi. You check inside yet?"

"Yeah, everything's pretty much in one piece," he said, his gaze drifting to the crack she'd been examining. "That looks like it could be fixed up easily. A bit of mortar should do the trick."

Capri nodded, relieved. "Could've been worse, I guess. How's your place?"

Bodhi shrugged. "Fine, but Alyssa's another story. The quake totally wigged her out. She's from Seattle, so she's no stranger to earthquakes, and this didn't help."

Capri raised an eyebrow. "Alyssa's here? When did your girl-friend arrive?"

"She got in late last night," he said, rubbing the back of his neck. "She joked about not even unpacking, just in case there's another quake. That way, she can make a quick exit if she decides to bail on this place."

Capri couldn't help but smirk. "Not exactly the welcome she was expecting, huh?"

"Nope," Bodhi answered with a chuckle, though there was a hint of frustration in his tone. "I had to bribe her with promises of a nonstop supply of chocolate and foot rubs just to keep her from bolting. Not sure how long that's gonna hold her, though."

Capri offered a small smile. "Yeah, rugged mountain land-scapes are not for everyone. This place can be a little unpre-dictable, but that's what makes it home."

Bodhi nodded, glancing toward their beloved Tetons. "Yeah, true—but I'd take Thunder Mountain over Seattle any day."

Capri glanced back at the crack in the wall. "I'll grab some supplies and patch this up later today. We've got enough on our hands without letting a little crack turn into something bigger."

"Good call," Bodhi said, giving her a nod. "I'll be around if you need a hand."

"Thanks," Capri replied, her mind already shifting gears as she thought about what else needed to be done. "I'm going to head into town, see how things are holding up there."

"Let me know if you learn anything—I'm here to help," Bodhi said as she started toward her truck.

"Will do," she called back, giving him a wave before climbing in and heading down the road.

As she drove into Thunder Mountain, Capri noticed the subtle changes the quake had left behind. The town was quieter than usual, the normal busy activity replaced with an uneasy calm. People were out on the streets, checking on their homes and businesses, their faces tight with concern.

She parked near the Rustic Pine and stepped out of her red truck, taking a moment to breathe in the crisp mountain air. Despite the damage, there was a resilience in the town, a determination to keep moving forward no matter what.

She started to walk down the main street, taking in the scene—some buildings had suffered minor damage, nothing catastrophic, but enough to remind everyone just how vulnerable they were.

Her eyes landed on the Town Hall, standing proud despite a few new cracks in its stone foundation. A small group had gathered outside, their heads bent in conversation. Fleet Southcott, the town sheriff, was there, his hands on his hips, a determined look on his face as he spoke to a couple of townsfolk. They were probably discussing the damage, figuring out how to repair what had been broken.

Capri hesitated for a moment, then made her way over. "Hey, everyone. That was quite the quake, wasn't it?"

Albie Barton, the town's ever-enthusiastic newspaper reporter, perked up immediately. "Capri! Can you believe it? Finally, some real news! I can already see the front page now.

He lifted his fingers in air quotes. "*Thunder Mountain Quakes —Town Rocks, But the Residents Roll With It!*"

Capri laughed, appreciating his much-needed sense of humor. "I'm sure you'll do the story justice, Albie."

Oma Griffith shuffled onto the scene, her ever-present lawn chair in hand and explaining that she had just come from the cemetery, where she spent the past hours chatting with her dearly departed husband, filling him in on all the latest about the earthquake and how the shaking toppled Noah's Ark.

"I told him all about it," she announced to the group with a twinkle in her eye, setting her chair down with a determined thump. "Earl always did love a good bit of excitement, and this event was a doozy."

Capri's phone buzzed in her pocket. Pulling it out, she saw Jake's name on the screen. A grin immediately formed.

Unfortunately, his brief message made her heart sink. *Just got some bad news. The earthquake has caused an unexpected demand for building supplies. Work's going to be delayed. I'll keep you posted.*

She stared at the text for a moment, disappointment settling over her. It wasn't just the delay in the renovations that bothered her—though that was frustrating enough—it was the realization that she wouldn't be seeing Jake again as soon as she'd hoped. She hadn't comprehended just how much she was looking forward to his next visit.

With a sigh, Capri slipped her phone back into her pocket, trying to shake off the disappointment. "Guess I'm the one who will just have to roll with it," she muttered, though the thought of waiting left the words feeling hollow.

Oma Griffith, ever observant, noticed the shadow that crossed Capri's face. "Something on your mind, dear?" she asked, her voice soft with concern.

Capri forced a smile. "Just got word there's going to be a delay with some house renovations," she said, keeping her tone light. "I was really hoping to get things moving, that's all."

Albie turned his attention to her. "Renovations?"

She nodded. "Yeah, since Mom has moved and it's just me now, I thought it might be a good time to update the cabin."

Oma nodded sympathetically. "Delays are never easy, especially when you've got your heart set on something," she said.

Capri simply nodded, grateful that Oma didn't press further. Some things were better left unsaid.

16

Capri parked her truck at the Lupine Meadows trailhead, one of her favorite spots in the Grand Tetons. The early morning light filtered through the towering pines, casting long shadows across the ground. She took a deep breath of the crisp mountain air, the scent of pine and earth filling her lungs. The world was quiet, save for the occasional rustle of leaves and the distant call of a bird. It was the perfect place to clear her head before heading to work and a full day of raft tours.

She slipped off her sandals and reached for her running shoes in the back seat. After lacing them up, Capri grabbed her water bottle and bear spray, tucking both into the side pockets of her running vest, before setting off down the trail.

The path ahead wound through a thick forest of fir and aspen, the underbrush dotted with wildflowers in shades of purple and yellow. The Lupine Meadows trail was well-worn, a familiar friend she had run countless times before, leading up toward a lake with a majestic mountain backdrop that could take one's breath away.

She needed that today—to focus on the grandeur of creation. Somehow, it made her concerns feel small.

The trail started to incline, and Capri pushed herself harder, her breathing growing more labored as she powered up the hill. The morning sun began to rise higher, dappling the forest floor with patches of light. She reached a bend in the trail where the trees thinned out, giving her a stunning view of the Teton Range, their jagged peaks still dusted with snow even in early summer.

She stopped, leaned over, and placed her hands on her knees to catch her breath. Seconds later, she straightened and absorbed the beauty of the scene—one she would never tire of gazing upon.

Capri continued down the trail, the solitude of the backcountry wrapped around her like a comforting embrace. Out here, with nothing but the sound of her footsteps and the whisper of the trees, the chaos of life faded into the background, leaving her with a rare, peaceful clarity and resolve.

Sure, she had faced plenty of losses lately, but she was determined to be resilient. She'd spent enough time sniveling like a heartbroken teenager, and that wasn't who she was. Despite the emotional upheaval of the past few weeks, she knew she was far stronger than that—a woman who could endure any storm with her head held high and her heart unwavering. It just took her a little longer this time to regain her footing, that's all.

Her feet pounded the ground a little faster as that thought took hold.

As Capri rounded another bend in the trail, the smell of sizzling bacon hit her nose, making her stomach rumble. Just off the path, a group of backcountry campers had set up their site, a small fire crackling as they cooked breakfast. One of the campers, a guy with a wide-brimmed hat and a friendly smile, lifted a hand in greeting.

"Morning!" he called out, flipping the bacon in the pan.

Capri returned the wave, offering a brief smile as she jogged past. The scent of bacon lingered in the air, mingling with the fresh pine and earth, a comforting reminder of simple pleasures.

As Capri continued her steady jog, her mind began to churn with thoughts from the day before. The conversation with Jake about the delay in getting building materials replayed in her head, and the frustration threatened to bubble up again.

She quickly tamped down her rising irritation and forced herself to focus on the rhythm of her breathing instead.

As she settled into her stride, Capri's thoughts drifted to the crack in the cinderblock wall at work. It wasn't a major issue, but it was a reminder of how things had fractured around her. But this—this she could fix. Determined, she resolved to take care of it the moment she got there, one small thing she could chalk up to a victory.

Capri's legs burned as she pushed herself beyond her usual pace, the pounding rhythm of her feet matching the intensity of her racing mind. She welcomed the physical strain, letting it clear her head and ground her in the moment.

Suddenly, the path beneath her feet gave a slight tremble. Capri stopped in her tracks, heart pounding, as the earth shuddered briefly. It was a small aftershock, but strong enough to dislodge a few rocks from the nearby slope. She watched as they tumbled down, bouncing off the trail with sharp clatters before settling in the brush below.

Capri stood still, her pulse quickening, waiting for any sign of another tremor. When the ground remained calm, she exhaled slowly, feeling a renewed sense of resolve settle over her.

The aftershock was done, and so was the moment of hesitation.

With her mind clear and her resurrected conviction firmly

in place, Capri resumed her run, letting the rhythm of her steps propel her forward. By the time she reached the end of the trail, she had a plan. She knew exactly what needed to be done.

She drove straight to work, determination fueling her every move. As she arrived at the building, her eyes immediately sought out the crack in the cinderblock wall. Without hesitation, she grabbed her tools, ready to take care of it herself.

Capri knelt beside the cinderblock wall, the mid-morning light casting long shadows across the rough surface. The crack was narrow but ran jaggedly along the length of several blocks, a small yet visible reminder of the recent tremors. She ran her fingers along the gap, feeling the uneven edges, her mind already calculating the steps needed to mend it.

Grabbing a trowel and a bucket of mortar, she set to work, mixing the mortar with just the right amount of water until it reached a thick, paste-like consistency. With steady hands, she began applying the mixture to the crack, smoothing it over the damaged area with careful, precise strokes. The repetitive motion was calming, grounding her as she filled in the open space, her mind focused solely on the task at hand.

As she finished the first layer, she heard footsteps approaching. Glancing over her shoulder, she saw Bodhi walking toward her, his easygoing demeanor evident in the relaxed sway of his gait. He stopped a few feet away, hands in his pockets, watching her work with a curious expression.

"Didn't know you were moonlighting as a mason," he teased, a grin tugging at the corner of his mouth.

Capri glanced up at him, wiping a bead of sweat from her forehead with the back of her hand. "Gotta be a jack-of-all-trades around here," she replied, her tone light. "Besides, I wasn't about to let this crack sit here and get worse."

Bodhi nodded, looking at the wall. "Need any help?"

Capri shook her head, a faint smile playing on her lips. "I've got it under control. Just a little touch-up, really. But I appreciate the offer."

He leaned against the side of the building, crossing his arms. "Have it your way, boss."

Capri focused on smoothing out the last bit of mortar, feeling a sense of satisfaction as the crack disappeared beneath her careful work. "Sometimes it's just easier to fix things yourself," she said, her voice steady.

Bodhi tilted his head, studying her for a moment. "You know, it's okay to let others lend a hand—it doesn't make you any less capable."

Capri looked up, meeting his gaze with a thoughtful expression. "I'll keep that in mind," she replied, her tone softening. "But for now, I think I've got this one covered."

With the crack filled and the wall looking as good as new, Capri stood up, brushing the dust off her hands. Bodhi gave her an approving nod, his grin widening. "Looks solid. You did good, Capri."

"Thanks," she said, feeling a quiet sense of accomplishment. "One less thing to worry about."

As Bodhi pushed off the wall and turned to leave, he glanced back with a grin. "Don't go hogging all the fun—leave some work for the rest of us."

Capri watched him walk away, a small smile lingering on her lips. Maybe he was right—there was no harm in accepting help now and then. But for now, she was content knowing she was a strong woman fully capable of handling things on her own.

17

Capri tightened the last strap on the raft, giving it a firm tug before stepping back to survey her work. The sun was already high, casting long shadows from the towering pine trees that surrounded the transport vehicle. The sound of the river in the distance was a constant reminder of the day ahead, filled with eager tourists looking for adventure.

"Bodhi!" she called out, her voice cutting through the morning air. "Make sure you keep an eye on those new rock croppings around the bend after the second set of rapids. The earthquake shifted things a bit, and I don't want anyone getting caught off guard."

Bodhi nodded, his long hair falling into his face as he slung a coil of rope over his shoulder. "Got it, Cap. I'll take it slow around that section."

"Good," Capri said, wiping her hands on her jeans. She tilted her head in the direction of the passengers standing several yards away. "Remember, safety first. If anything feels off, pull back and reassess. We don't need any heroics out there."

"Got it," he said, the look he gave her a silent reminder of the run they'd made together—where Capri had pushed the limits a bit. He started to open his mouth to say more when she interrupted. "Let's not go there," she warned.

Bodhi responded with a simple grin as he moved to finish loading the rest of the gear, while Capri checked her clipboard, mentally ticking off the list of tasks still to be done. She walked over to the trailer, checking the oars, life vests, and helmets, ensuring everything was in place.

Just as she bent down to double-check the first aid kit, her phone buzzed in her back pocket. She pulled it out, seeing Jake Carrington's name on the screen. Her heart did a small flip before she could stop it.

"Secured some supplies," the text read. "They won't be in for a couple of days, but I've drawn up some preliminary plans. Would like to review them with you."

Capri stared at the screen, a rush of elation threatening to break through her carefully constructed defenses.

"Sounds good," she quickly typed back. "Let's meet out at the cabin later this afternoon. Say, four o'clock?"

A thumbs-up icon appeared.

She slipped the phone back into her pocket, her fingers lingering on it for just a moment longer than necessary. Taking a deep breath, Capri turned her attention back to the tasks at hand, her mind already beginning to plan out the rest of her day.

"Alright, Bodhi," she called out, her voice steady and authoritative. "Let's get this show on the road."

Just like that, the summer rafting season began.

AFTER A WHIRLWIND DAY filled with activity, Capri returned to her cabin, the noise of the day still echoing in her mind. She stood on the porch, the late afternoon sun casting long shadows across the yard as she watched Jake's truck rumble up the gravel drive, a small cloud of dust trailing behind.

The place felt different now, quieter since her mother had moved out. While the looming renovations created a level of excitement, she admitted to herself she had mixed feelings. The prospect of changes to the home she'd always known left a knot of uncertainty in her stomach.

Jake parked and stepped out, a stack of rolled-up blueprints under one arm. He offered her a nod, his calm demeanor in place as if they were about to discuss something as mundane as the weather. Part of her appreciated that steadiness, even if it annoyed her at the same time.

"Afternoon," he greeted, making his way up the steps to the porch.

"Hey," she replied, folding her arms as she leaned against the porch railing. "So, let's see what you came up with."

Jake didn't seem fazed by her brusque tone. He simply unrolled the first blueprint on the small outdoor table, using a couple of rocks to hold down the corners. "After our initial talk, I've got a few ideas for you," he began, spreading out the rest of the plans so she could see.

Capri glanced down at the paper, trying to ignore the way her pulse quickened slightly. "What's this?" she asked, pointing to a section of the layout.

Jake followed her finger, his voice steady as he explained. "This is the kitchen. I know you mentioned keeping it mostly the same, but I was thinking we could add an island here. It would give you more counter space and improve the flow."

She frowned, shaking her head. "I don't need an island. It's been fine without one."

"I get that," Jake said, his tone calm. "But adding an island would make the kitchen more functional. It's a small change, but it could make cooking and entertaining easier. Plus, it wouldn't take away from the cozy feel you want to keep."

Capri huffed, crossing her arms tightly. "Seems like a waste of money to me. As I said before, money is no object. But I don't like squandering any of the budget, either."

Jake didn't argue. Instead, he nodded thoughtfully. "We can stick with the current layout if you prefer. I just wanted to present the option. Sometimes it's worth considering a little extra functionality."

She didn't respond, simply gesturing for him to continue. He took out another sheet, this one detailing the living area.

"If you open up this wall, it will create a more open concept and allow more light in," he said, tapping the blueprint. "You'd still have distinct areas for living and dining, but with a better, and more modern, flow."

Capri immediately shook her head. "Absolutely not. That existing wall makes the space feel cozy."

Jake was unflappable. "I understand. But think about it this way—by opening it up, you'd make the space feel larger, more welcoming. We could add a partial divider or bookcase to keep some separation if that's important to you, without losing the benefits of an open layout."

Her annoyance flared again. "I like the space the way it is, Jake. This isn't some fancy showroom."

Jake leaned back slightly, giving her room to breathe. "I hear you. But cozy doesn't have to mean closed off. It's about balance. This change could make a big difference in how the space feels, especially in the long run."

Surprisingly, Capri felt herself growing more frustrated with each suggestion. "What else?"

Jake pulled out another drawing, this one showing the exterior. "The front porch—right now, it's functional, but I think we could enhance it a bit. Maybe extend it slightly, make it a more inviting entrance while still keeping the original character."

Capri studied the sketch, her fingers tracing the outline of the porch. "I don't want it to look too new. This place has history."

Never mind she'd originally suggested bulldozing the entire cabin. She had a right to change her mind, and all these alterations seemed daunting and unnecessary.

Jake nodded, his voice soothing. "Absolutely. We'd use materials that match the original as closely as possible—weathered wood, traditional fixtures. It would keep all the charm it has now, just with a bit more usability and appeal. A place where you could sit, enjoy the view, maybe entertain."

She couldn't help but feel a small tug of interest, despite herself. "It better not stick out like a sore thumb."

"It won't," Jake assured her, his eyes meeting hers with a sincerity that was hard to argue with. "I promise."

They went over more details—the structural changes, necessary updates to plumbing, and even a new paint scheme. Each time, Capri found herself resisting, questioning his choices as if testing his tolerance for compromise. But Jake never wavered. He explained everything clearly, patiently, as if her objections were expected, maybe even welcomed.

By the time they finished, the sun was dipping low in the sky, casting the yard in golden light. Capri let out a long breath, feeling both exhausted and strangely content. Despite all her pushback, she knew in her gut that Jake's suggestions made sense.

Capri couldn't deny that Jake had a steady hand and a clear head, qualities she valued in anyone she worked with. He wasn't easily rattled, and that quiet confidence spoke volumes. He didn't push his ideas arrogantly; instead, he presented them logically, leaving room for discussion.

It was also clear he knew his craft, and though she wasn't one to hand out respect easily, Jake had managed to earn a bit of hers through sheer competence and unwavering resolve.

"Fine," she said finally, with a touch of resignation. "We'll go with your plans—all of them. But if I don't like something, I'll be voicing it."

Jake's smile was genuine, a soft curve that made something in her chest tighten. "I wouldn't expect anything less."

As she watched him roll up the blueprints, ready to head out, Capri couldn't shake the feeling that maybe, just maybe, she was starting to trust him. And that, more than anything, was what made her nervous.

18

Reva stood near the entrance of the Thunder Mountain Community Center, watching as the townspeople filled the space, their footsteps echoing off the polished wood floors. The wide windows along one wall offered a stunning view of the Teton Range, their jagged edges cutting sharply into the early evening sky.

Rows of chairs had been arranged in neat lines facing the front, where a small dais had been set up for the evening's meeting. It was a simple space, but the high ceilings and exposed beams gave it a welcoming, open feel.

Reva made her way to the front where a small podium was already positioned with a microphone. She caught sight of Capri, Charlie Grace, and Lila sitting together near the middle, their heads close as they chatted quietly. The air was thick with anticipation, a mix of curiosity and unease about the recent earthquakes that had rattled the town.

Once everyone had settled, Reva stepped up to the podium and tapped the microphone to get the room's attention. The hum of conversation died down as the townspeople turned their eyes toward her.

"Good evening, everyone," Reva began, her voice steady but warm. "Thank you all for coming tonight. I know the recent earthquakes have raised a lot of concerns, and that's why we've brought in an expert to help us understand what's going on."

She gestured toward the man standing to her left, his presence commanding without being imposing. "This is Dr. Grant Marshall, a geologist from the University of Wyoming with extensive experience in seismic activity, particularly in regions like ours. He's here to explain the situation, answer your questions, and hopefully ease some of the worries we've all been feeling."

Dr. Marshall stepped forward, nodding appreciatively as Reva moved aside. The overhead lights reflected off his glasses as he unrolled a large map of the Teton area, pinning it to an easel next to the podium. His calm demeanor seemed to settle the room as he began.

"Thank you, Mayor Nygard," he started, his voice resonant and clear. "Good evening, everyone. I know you've had quite a few surprises lately, so let's talk about what's happening beneath your feet."

He pointed to the map, tracing the fault line that ran along the base of the Teton Range. "The Teton Fault is what's responsible for the earthquakes you've been experiencing. It's a normal fault, meaning it's caused by the earth's crust being pulled apart. This kind of fault is common in areas where the tectonic plates are moving away from each other."

Reva glanced around the room, noting the mix of expressions—some concerned, others simply curious. The newly built center was proving its worth tonight, offering a comfortable space for this important discussion.

"But what about Yellowstone?" came a voice from the back, belonging to Albie Barton, the town's ever-inquisitive newspaper reporter. He pulled a fountain pen from his pocket protector and prepared to take notes on his clipboard. "Isn't that supervolcano gonna blow someday?"

Dr. Marshall smiled slightly, nodding as if he had expected the question. "Yellowstone is indeed a supervolcano, and it does experience seismic activity. However, the tremors you've been feeling here are not directly related to Yellowstone's volcanic system. The Teton Fault and Yellowstone are part of the same broader tectonic system, but they operate independently. The earthquakes you're experiencing are localized to the Teton area."

Reva noticed Capri leaning over to whisper something to Charlie Grace, who responded with a quick nod. They were all paying close attention, but she could see that some of the initial tension in their faces was beginning to ease.

"What are the chances of a bigger quake hitting us?" another voice asked, this time from Thelma DeRosier, their beloved bank teller and a long-time resident with a reputation for worrying about worst-case scenarios.

Dr. Marshall paused, choosing his words carefully. "While we can't predict earthquakes with absolute certainty, the Teton Fault is capable of producing larger quakes. However, significant events are rare and occur over long periods—every 2,000 to 4,000 years on average. The tremors you've been feeling are more likely to be smaller adjustments—some are aftershocks rather than precursors to a larger event."

Reva caught Lila's eye and gave her a reassuring nod. Lila smiled faintly in return, though Reva could tell she was still thinking about the "what ifs."

A hand shot up from the middle of the room—Larry York, the local conspiracy theorist. "Could the government be doing underground military tests, causing these quakes? We've all heard the stories."

Dr. Marshall maintained his composure, though there was a flicker of amusement in his eyes. "No, sir. These earthquakes are entirely natural. Like I explained, they're caused by tectonic forces and the release of stress along fault lines. There's no evidence to suggest that any man-made activities, including government tests, are involved in these events."

Larry York shot up from his seat, his face lit with the thrill of another wild idea. "But what if it's Bigfoot stomping around up there? You know those Sasquatches have been known to shake the ground when they're mad!"

Dr. Marshall blinked, clearly struggling to keep a straight face. "I assure you, Mister..."

"York. Larry York."

"Yes, Mr. York. I assure you, if Bigfoot were causing seismic activity, we'd have far more to worry about than just earthquakes."

"Well, son of a hairy pig's butt, I hope you're right." Larry's face immediately reddened. "I apologize, I didn't mean to swear."

Dr. Marshall shook his head and grinned. "I'm not sure you did."

A ripple of laughter moved through the room, breaking some of the tension that had been hanging in the air. Reva could see a few shoulders relaxing, and even Capri allowed herself a small smile.

"Could fracking in nearby areas be responsible?" Betty Dunning asked, genuine concern in her voice.

Dr. Marshall shook his head slightly. "While fracking can induce seismic activity, the operations in nearby states are too far from the Teton Fault to have any significant impact here. What you're feeling is the result of natural tectonic processes, not human activities."

The discussion continued for a while longer, with questions ranging from practical concerns about earthquake prepared-ness to more far-fetched theories about ancient curses and hidden fault lines. The professor answered each one with the same calm, measured tone, never dismissive but always clear.

"In short," he concluded, "earthquakes are a natural part of living in a region like this. The earth's surface is constantly shifting, and while that can be unsettling, it's also something we can prepare for. With the right precautions and an understanding of the risks, you can keep yourselves and your community safe."

Reva stepped forward to thank Dr. Marshall, feeling a sense of relief that the meeting had gone well. As the townspeople began to disperse, she turned to her friends, who were already gathering their things.

"Well," Capri said, stretching her arms above her head, "that was...informative."

"And not as scary as I thought it'd be," Lila added, a note of relief in her voice.

"Still," Charlie Grace said, tucking her notebook under her arm. "We should all be prepared, just in case."

Reva nodded in agreement, feeling a renewed sense of responsibility for her town. "We will be," she said with quiet determination. "And we'll get through this together, just like we always do."

As they left the community center, Reva glanced back at the room, now nearly empty but still filled with the echoes of the evening's conversation. She felt a little more at ease, reassured by the shared resolve she'd seen in her neighbors' faces.

Thunder Mountain was ready for whatever Mother Nature decided to throw their way next.

19

C apri texted her mom numerous times over the course of days. Finally, she received a reply. "Sorry, honey. We've been so busy. As of last Tuesday, I am officially Mrs. Earl Dunlop. After several days of fun in Vegas, we'll be driving to Idaho over the weekend. Here's a few pics of the wedding."

Capri scrolled through several images of her mother and Earl in some wedding chapel posing with Elvis. She rolled her eyes and closed the message, then wandered out and sat on the porch, her legs stretched out in front of her, the wooden boards rough beneath her bare feet. The evening air was crisp, with a slight breeze carrying the scent of pine and sagebrush.

Normally, sitting here brought her peace, but tonight her mind was a jumble of thoughts she couldn't untangle. Her mother's sudden marriage and move to Idaho felt like a jolt, leaving Capri with a hollow ache she hadn't expected. She'd spent so long being her mother's rock, the fixer of things, the one to keep it all together. Now, without that tether, she felt adrift, uncertain of her own place.

She sighed and leaned her head back against the porch rail,

her eyes drifting over the silhouette of the mountains. Her friends had all found their footing lately—Charlie Grace with her photography exhibit and Nick Thatcher. Lila running the vet clinic with Whit Calloway, and Reva balancing her work as mayor, raising Lucan, and enjoying her new role as wife to Kellen Warner.

They had each found something, and someone, to hold onto. Capri wasn't bitter, but she felt like the odd one out, stuck in place while everyone else moved forward.

Her phone buzzed beside her, breaking the stillness. She glanced down, her heart skipping when she saw the name on the screen: Jake Carrington. The contractor she'd hired to work on her mother's old cabin had texted a few times since they met, keeping her updated on supplies and project details. Nothing personal, just business—but still, she found herself hesitating before opening the message.

"Got more of the materials in. Enough to get started. Want to meet tomorrow to go over the final schedule?"

Straightforward, no extra words. That was Jake. Capri let out a breath she hadn't realized she was holding. He was reliable, the kind of guy who did what he said he would, no nonsense. It was refreshing, especially after the whirlwind of the last few months. She admired that about him, though she barely knew him.

"Sure. What time?" she typed back, her thumb lingering over the send button for a second longer than necessary.

Almost immediately, his reply came: "Noon? I'll bring the plans."

She sent a thumbs-up emoji, then dropped her phone back onto the porch and stared out into the darkening sky. She should be excited about the cabin renovations, but there was something about the whole situation that unsettled her. Maybe it was Jake himself—steady and confident.

They'd only just met, yet his presence had already stirred

something inside her she couldn't quite name. It wasn't romantic, at least not yet, but there was a quiet connection, a sense that he didn't just see the surface of things. And that was the problem—because if he looked too closely, he might see that Capri didn't have it all together, that she wasn't as confident or sure of herself as she pretended to be.

Her phone buzzed again. Another text from Jake.

"Looking forward to it."

Capri blinked at the message. Just four words, but they sent a ripple through her. She shouldn't be overthinking it. It was just a meeting, just plans for the cabin. Still, something in the back of her mind kept her on edge, as if meeting him again might tip the balance of her carefully ordered life.

With a sigh, she stood up, stretching out her stiff muscles. The evening air had grown colder, and she wrapped her arms around herself as she took one last look at the mountains. Tomorrow would come soon enough, and with it, more decisions. For now, she allowed herself a brief moment of quiet, hoping it would settle the unease Jake's message had stirred inside her.

The next day, just before noon, Capri wandered out onto her porch, a half-eaten bologna sandwich in hand. She heard the crunch of gravel and looked up to see Jake pulling up in his truck. He waved through the windshield before stepping out, the plans rolled up in one hand, the other holding a thermos of what she assumed was coffee. He looked as solid as ever, dressed in a worn flannel and work boots, like he belonged here among the mountains and wild landscape.

"Afternoon," he called, his voice easy and steady, just like the man himself. He met her halfway up the path, his familiar smile in place. "Hope I didn't keep you waiting."

"No, just got here myself after being in town all morning. Things are ramping up with tourist season and all," Capri explained, trying to ignore the small flutter in her chest at the sight of him. She crossed her arms, more to give herself something to do than to ward off the chill. "So, what's the plan?"

Jake unrolled the plans on the hood of his truck, holding them down with a couple of rocks. Capri stepped closer, standing shoulder to shoulder with him as he explained each detail—his final suggestions for updating the kitchen, reinforcing the foundation, and reworking the back porch. His voice was smooth and calm, a stark contrast to the whirlwind of thoughts racing in her head.

"You okay with this layout?" Jake asked, glancing over at her.

Capri blinked, realizing she hadn't been paying attention. "Yeah. Sorry. What did you say about the porch again?"

Jake didn't seem fazed by her distraction. He tapped the plan with his finger. "I was thinking we could expand it a bit, give you more space to sit out and enjoy the view. It wouldn't take much work to extend the decking."

Capri nodded, trying to focus. "That sounds good. I mean, you're the expert. I trust your judgment."

The words felt strange on her tongue and were contradictory to their first encounter.

Trust.

She wasn't sure why she said it—it wasn't like they knew each other well enough for that. But Jake smiled, that easygoing, steady smile that made her feel both at ease and on edge at the same time.

"Glad to hear it," he said. "I'd like to start tomorrow if that's alright."

"Great." Capri stepped back, putting a little more space between them. She caught herself chewing the inside of her cheek, an old habit that showed up whenever she felt unsure of something. "I guess I'll leave it in your hands then."

Jake's gaze lingered on her for a moment, his eyes steady

but thoughtful, like he was reading more into her words than she'd meant to reveal. "I'll take care of it. No worries."

Capri nodded, but there was something in the way he said it—so certain, so unwavering. Why did his confidence throw her? This wasn't personal; it was just business. So why did she feel like there was more to it than that?

"Well," she said, taking another step away from him. "I should get going. Got a lot on my plate today."

Jake didn't push. He just gave a nod and started rolling up the plans. "I'll get started in the morning. You can let me know if anything changes on your end."

"Will do." She walked him around his truck, but the moment they reached the driver's door, Jake's voice stopped her.

"Capri."

She paused. "Yeah?"

"If there's ever anything else you need—about the cabin or otherwise—just let me know. I'm around."

There was nothing particularly loaded in the way he said it. But his offer made something twist in her chest, a discomfort she couldn't explain.

"Thanks," she managed, watching while he climbed into the driver's seat and pulled away.

As he drove down the lane leading to the highway, Capri couldn't stop replaying the conversation in her head. Jake hadn't done anything to warrant the strange anxiety simmering beneath her skin, but it was there all the same, a quiet nagging at the back of her mind. She shook it off, focusing on the tasks ahead.

Besides, it was nothing. Jake was simply being the ultimate professional.

But deep down, Capri knew that wasn't entirely true.

20

J ake arrived early the next morning, his truck rumbling into the driveway. Capri stood on the porch, waiting, arms crossed against the cool morning air. She had packed up most of the items in the cabin to accommodate the renovation, and the living room was now a maze of boxes, each one labeled with a Sharpie scrawl.

"Morning," Jake said as he hopped out of the truck, giving her a quick nod before grabbing his tool belt from the passenger seat.

"Morning," Capri replied, pushing a stray lock of hair behind her ear. She led him inside, weaving through the boxes with an ease that came from days of packing. "I've got most of it cleared out, but there's still some stuff to move."

Jake's gaze landed on one of the boxes, his brow furrowing. "*Gilmore Girls?*" he asked, sounding both surprised and amused.

Capri looked over and saw the familiar handwriting on the side of the box. She laughed, a little embarrassed. "Yeah. My stepdad and I used to watch these DVDs together. It's kind of our thing."

Jake raised an eyebrow. "No kidding? You're looking at one of Stars Hollow's biggest fans right here."

Capri blinked. "Wait, what? You watch *Gilmore Girls*?"

Jake chuckled, clearly entertained by her reaction. "I grew up with two sisters, and it was either learn to love Lorelai and Rory or get stuck watching home makeover shows. I chose *Gilmore Girls*."

Capri smirked, shaking her head. "I don't know whether to be impressed or worried."

"I'll take impressed," Jake said with a grin, stepping over to help her lift the box. "Where do you want this?"

"Upstairs, against the wall in the bedroom," she replied, trying not to notice how effortlessly he hoisted the box. She led him up the stairs, her stomach doing a little flip as they entered the bedroom. It was mostly bare now, save for the bed, dresser, and a few stray items that hadn't been packed away.

As Jake set the box down, Capri felt a strange tension in the air. She wasn't used to having anyone in her personal space like this, especially not someone who seemed to fill the room so effortlessly. She busied herself with grabbing another box from the hallway, acutely aware of how closely Jake moved behind her.

He straightened up, looking around the room. "Nice space. Lots of light."

Capri nodded, avoiding his eyes. "Yeah. It's a good spot."

The silence stretched just long enough to make her feel a little flustered. "I'll show you what I packed up from the kitchen," she said quickly, motioning for him to follow her downstairs. She heard his footsteps behind her, measured and unhurried, and that odd awareness of him hadn't quite faded by the time they reached the bottom.

Jake rolled up his sleeves, surveying the downstairs space with a practical eye. "Before we get to rebuilding, we've got to tear some things down. Old wood's gotta come out, especially in the kitchen. Apologies in advance for the mess—it'll look worse before it looks better, but it won't last long."

Capri shrugged, hands on her hips. "I'll survive."

Jake chuckled, his eyes glinting with amusement. "That's the spirit."

With that, he got to work, and Capri headed out the back door into her mother's garden. It was overgrown, in need of weeding, but she could still spot the bright green heads of lettuce peeking through the soil. She figured she'd busy herself with pulling weeds and cleaning the bedding areas.

She crouched down, pulling at clumps of crabgrass and dandelions with focused determination. The earthy smell of the garden was comforting. A little too comforting, perhaps, because she didn't notice the soft rustle in the bushes behind her.

Until it was too late.

The sharp, unmistakable scent hit her before she even turned around. A skunk—stark black and white—stood just a few feet away, its tail raised high like a warning flag. Capri froze, eyes wide. "No, no, no—"

But it was too late. The spray hit her with precision, an acrid stench that immediately made her gag.

"Are you kidding me?!" she groaned, stumbling backward, trying to cover her nose as the smell sank into her clothes, her hair—everything. She heard the sound of the back door creaking open and turned to see Jake standing there, his sleeves rolled up and wearing an expression that was a mix of amusement and concern.

"Capri... you, uh... okay over there?"

She threw up her hands in defeat. "Does it look like I'm okay?!"

Jake bit back a laugh, plugging his nose with his fingers. "Just checking. You might want to... take care of that."

Capri glared at him, though the corners of her mouth twitched. "You think?"

He crossed his arms, leaning casually against the door-frame. "I'd offer to help, but I'm pretty sure my nose can't take it."

She continued to stare at him, incredulous, as the smell worsened with each passing second. "Jake Carrington, if you don't quit laughing—"

But before she could finish, a laugh escaped him, deep and unrestrained. And despite herself, Capri joined in, the absurdity of the situation too much to resist.

"You're lucky I don't make you take a tomato bath too," she grumbled, wiping her face with the back of her hand.

Jake just grinned, his eyes still twinkling. "I think you've got this one covered. I'll just... stay upwind."

CAPRI STEPPED out of the shower, her skin still tingling from scrubbing what felt like every inch of herself. She'd used every trick in the book—tomato juice, baking soda, even vinegar— but no matter how much she tried, the faint scent of skunk still clung to her like a persistent shadow she couldn't shake.

Wrapping a towel around herself, she glanced in the mirror and sighed. Plans for lunch with Jake were clearly off the table now. No way was she going to sit through a meal smelling like this, no matter how faint.

Still, she dressed and headed downstairs, only to find Jake wiping down the countertops where he had started clearing debris.

"You good?" he asked with an easy smile, his eyes twinkling as he glanced at her.

Capri shrugged, wrinkling her nose. "As good as I'm gonna be. I still smell like a skunk."

Jake leaned against the counter, arms crossed. "I've been around worse. You up for lunch?"

Capri blinked, surprised. "You... want to have lunch with me? I smell."

He chuckled. "Capri, I've been through muddy construction sites, knee-deep in goodness-knows-what. A little leftover skunk smell doesn't scare me. I bet you have some food in that refrigerator. How about we whip something up together? I'm starving."

She hesitated, but the idea of making lunch together was too tempting to pass up, especially when the alternative was sulking alone in her room over her lingering odor. "Alright," she said, grabbing a hair tie to pull her damp hair back. "But you're in charge of chopping. I can't be trusted with sharp objects right now."

Jake laughed again, and they moved around the kitchen, getting out the ingredients. Capri rummaged through the fridge, pulling out the lettuce, tomatoes, some cheese, and deli meat.

"I make a mean grilled cheese sandwich," Jake said, searching the cabinets, then pulling out a pan and setting it on the stove. "Back home in Alabama, my mom taught me a few tricks."

"Alabama, huh?" Capri said as she sliced the lettuce. "That's a long way from Jackson Hole."

Jake nodded, slicing a tomato with practiced ease. "Yeah, I miss it sometimes. Grew up on a farm with my brothers and sisters. But once I got into carpentry and architecture, I was drawn to the mountains. Something about building homes where the land shapes the design, you know?"

Capri glanced over at him, admiring the way his hands moved with such care. "And Jackson Hole? What brought you all the way out here?"

He flipped the sandwich in the pan. "Wanted a fresh start. I worked in Alabama for a while, but it never felt right. The Tetons, though...they called to me. The landscape, the work—it just fit. And here I am."

There was something about the way he spoke, with a quiet certainty that Capri found deeply attractive. He didn't have a complicated backstory or some grand plan for the future—he just followed what felt right. She admired that. She admired...him.

She swallowed, her thoughts drifting to his eyes—deep, kind, even-keeled. It was the first time she really let herself linger on the thought, how she liked the way he looked at her. How he made her feel seen, even in her most chaotic moments.

Dick once said, "Hair will turn gray, weight will change, teeth will fall out and bodies shrink with age. But the eyes...the eyes grow old with you."

She dared to meet Jake's gaze and found he was watching her now, too, with a hint of something she hadn't noticed before.

"You always wanted to be a builder?" she asked, trying to distract herself from the way her stomach was doing small somersaults.

"Yeah. I prefer renovations," he said, shrugging one shoulder. "There's something about taking things apart and putting them back together better than before. It's honest work. It's what I like."

Capri caught the way his words echoed what he was doing in her cabin—tearing down the old to rebuild something stronger. And it wasn't lost on her how similar that felt to her own life, except she wasn't quite sure how to put the pieces back together.

They finished making the sandwiches, adding a salad and some potato chips to their plates. Capri pulled out a couple of beers, and they sat at the small kitchen table, the scent of warm bread and melted cheese filling the air.

As they ate, Jake asked about her life—what brought her to Thunder Mountain, what she loved about running the rafting business. "I grew up here. Thunder Mountain is my home. These people are my extended family, especially my girlfriends."

She found herself talking easily, sharing stories about her friends and how much she adored the mountains. She told him about Charlie Grace, Reva, and Lila...how they'd remained tight over the years and how much that meant to her. "They know me...you know what I mean?"

Even as the words escaped her lips, she silently acknowledged that even they didn't know the entire her...the lonely part. No one knew that side.

Through it all, she became increasingly aware of Jake's interest in her. The way he leaned in slightly when she spoke, how his eyes lingered just a little longer than necessary, the softness in his voice when he asked her questions.

Capri knew what that meant—she wasn't oblivious. And the truth was, she liked it. She liked the way he looked at her, the way he was drawn to her in a quiet, steadfast way. It was different from what she was used to, and that both intrigued and unsettled her.

Over the years, she'd dated plenty. All casual. Lots of good times. But nothing—and no one—had ever penetrated the hard shell she'd built around her. She was lonely, yet couldn't seem to invite anyone in.

The question was...why?

And why was she risking seeing Jake differently?

The realization crept up on her, catching her off guard. She cleared her throat, abruptly pushing her chair back from the table. "I should clean up. There's still a lot of work to do in town. Bodhi will need my help before taking out the final group of rafters." She stood and gathered their half-empty glasses.

Jake raised an eyebrow, glancing at the dishes in her hand. "I can help."

Before she could protest, he was up and by her side, collecting their dishes. His hand brushed against hers as they reached for the same plate, and Capri felt a jolt shoot through her, a warmth spreading up her arm that made her heart skip a beat. For a moment, the world seemed to still, and she was acutely aware of the closeness between them, the gentle touch of his fingers against her skin.

Her breath caught, and she pulled her hand away quickly, setting the plates down on the counter with a clatter. "Thanks, but I've got it," she said, a little too quickly, turning her back to him as she busied herself at the sink.

But the touch lingered, and as she rinsed the dishes, she couldn't help but feel the rush of conflicting emotions swirl inside her. She wasn't ready for this—whatever *this* was. Yet, at the same time, part of her wasn't sure she wanted to let it slip away.

21

"Goodness! What is that smell?" Reva wrinkled her nose and pulled back from embracing Capri at the door.

Capri grunted. "Skunk. Yes, I got sprayed."

Lila, Charlie Grace, and Reva let out a chorus of laughter.

"Oh no!" Lila said. "I'm so sorry."

"Yikes!" Reva said. Despite her sympathetic expression, she didn't refrain from holding her nose. "Sorry...it's just that—"

Capri shook her head. "No, I get it. I stink."

Charlie Grace whipped out her phone. She thumbed the tiny screen, then scrolled. "Says here a mixture of liquid dish soap, hydrogen peroxide, and baking soda will do the trick. Have you tried that?"

Capri sighed and handed off her jacket to Lila, who hung it on a line of pegs mounted on her wall. "Yes. And every other trick known to man and woman."

"Well, if it's any consolation, the smell should only linger a couple of days," Lila said. "I can't tell you how many dogs are brought into the clinic after a tussle with a skunk...or a porcupine." She grinned. "Guarantee, that's worse."

Capri followed her girlfriends into the kitchen. "I'll do my best to avoid that sticky situation."

Based on their laughter, her pun didn't escape the girls as they grabbed their drinks from the counter.

Capri followed them back to the living room and took a place on a chair opposite the sofa where they sat, several feet away. "In other news, I finally heard from my mom. She seems blissfully happy, even though the slot machines were not kind to Earl in Vegas."

Reva raised an eyebrow. "I can't imagine our Earl embracing Sin City. He just doesn't seem the type."

Capri nodded. "Yeah, I'm learning a lot of things I didn't expect." Capri forced a laugh, shifting in her seat. "Like how quickly life can change after decades of staying the same."

Charlie Grace leaned forward, concern flickering in her eyes. "And how are you feeling about it all? About your mom moving on so fast?"

Capri shrugged, crossing her legs and resting her hands on the armrests. "Honestly, I'm just trying to adjust. Everything's in flux, and it's weird."

Lila, who'd been quiet until now, offered a sympathetic smile. "Change is hard, even when it's good."

"Yeah," Capri said softly, feeling the weight of her friends' concern. "But enough about that. What about you guys? How's everything post-quake?"

Reva leaned back, cradling her drink in her lap. "I swear, I'm more than ready to move past the tremor issue. I was in the middle of a town meeting when a dump truck rumbled past out front and Verna practically jumped out of her skin, thinking we were having another earthquake."

Lila laughed. "I bet she did. That woman is high-strung on a good day. What happened?"

"She burst out of her seat like the world was ending," Reva replied with a shake of her head. "Muttering about potential structural damage to the mayor's office, even though there wasn't a crack in sight. It took everything I had not to laugh. I reassured everyone in the meeting that Thunder Mountain wasn't about to split in half."

Charlie Grace grinned. "You mean Verna didn't run to Pastor Pete, begging him to organize another town-wide prayer vigil?"

"Oh, trust me, she tried!" Reva said, rolling her eyes. "But I talked her down. Barely."

Lila chimed in, smiling. "Speaking of Pastor Pete, he's set up a workday to clean up the church grounds. Everyone is gathering at Moose Chapel tomorrow to help out."

"I'll swing by," Charlie Grace offered. "We're pretty busy out at the ranch, but I'll make time to help."

Capri raised an eyebrow. "How's your photography exhibit coming along? I thought you'd be swamped with prepping for the Jackson Hole exhibition."

Charlie Grace let out a sigh, rubbing her temples. "I am. I've barely slept this week, trying to finalize which prints to showcase. Between that and balancing everything with our heavy guest load, I feel like I'm spinning in circles. Nick's been a huge help, though."

"Sounds like you're juggling a lot," Lila said, nodding. "It's tough when you're stretched so thin like that."

"You're telling me," Charlie Grace agreed. "I love the challenge, but man, sometimes I just want to crawl into bed and forget about all of it."

Capri shifted in her chair. "You and Nick seem to have a good balance, though."

Charlie Grace smiled. "We try. He's been super supportive. I think he's more excited for the exhibit than I am. Keeps reminding me to breathe."

"I get it," Lila muttered, glancing down at her drink. "Between running the clinic and Camille being home from college, it feels like my house is a never-ending mess. Whit's been a great partner at work, but honestly, I barely have time to keep up with everything."

Reva shot her a sympathetic look. "Me, too. Lucan's been bouncing off the walls lately. He won't sleep without every stuffed animal he owns piled on top of him. It's been exhausting."

"Is he okay, though?" Capri asked, concern softening her tone. "All of us are on edge a bit after those tremors."

"Oh, he's fine, just very active." Reva reached for some peanuts from the bowl on the coffee table.

They all nodded in agreement, the weight of the past few weeks settling over them for a moment. Each of them had busy lives, but some seasons seemed more difficult than others.

"Well," Lila said after a pause, "at least we're all managing. One way or another."

"True," Capri said, her voice thoughtful as she leaned back. "I guess we've all got our own version of chaos to deal with."

The conversation shifted as they each shared updates about their lives. Lila mentioned a few new patients at the clinic, including a raccoon with a broken leg, while Charlie Grace brought up she was considering holding a big barbecue bash at the ranch—perhaps over the July fourth weekend. Reva filled them in on the town's recovery efforts, but even amidst the talk of minor repairs, they found moments to laugh about the absurdity of it all.

As the conversation began to wind down, Capri took a sip of her drink and sighed. "Well, speaking of managing chaos, I've had my hands full with the house renovations."

Reva glanced over. "How's that going? Are you ready to tear your hair out yet?"

Capri shook her head, trying to stay casual. "No, no. Jake's been on top of everything."

Lila perked up. "Jake? The contractor?"

Capri reached for a pretzel. "Uh, yeah. He's handling the work." She tossed the pretzel in her mouth.

Charlie Grace's eyes gleamed with mischief. "I heard he's very nice to look at." She elbowed Lila, and they winked at each other.

Capri's cheeks flushed. She should have known her friends would twist the situation into something it was not. "No, it's not like that. He's just..." She swallowed. "...doing the work I hired him to do. I mean, he's been very helpful."

"Helpful, huh?" Reva grinned. "That sounds suspiciously like something more."

Capri huffed, knowing she'd opened the door. "Look, he's a good guy, but it's strictly professional. He's remodeling my house...that's all."

Lila raised an eyebrow. "Strictly professional? That's what they all say."

Reva leaned back, her eyes narrowing playfully as she smiled. "You know, Capri, sometimes the universe throws people in our path for a reason. A man in your life might just be what you need right now." She winked, adding with a grin, "Besides, the way you look when you talk about him...I'd say there's more to this than just house renovations."

Capri crossed her arms, but a small smile tugged at her lips. "You're all impossible."

The girls exchanged knowing looks, their laughter fading as Capri tried to wave off the attention. But as she sat there, a quiet settled over her. Despite her efforts to brush it aside, she couldn't ignore the spark of something new—something unsettling yet strangely comforting.

The idea of Jake lingered, not just as the man renovating her house, but as someone who had begun to find his way into the cracks of her carefully guarded world. Maybe her friends weren't wrong. Maybe it was time to stop holding everything at arm's length and let herself feel—whatever that might mean.

22

Capri was elbow-deep in engine grease when Jake's truck rumbled into the gravel lot outside her rafting company. The sun was high, beating down on her as she worked, her wrench twisting stubbornly at a bolt that refused to budge. She wiped her brow with the back of her hand, squinting as she watched Jake hop out of the driver's seat.

"What brings you by?" she asked, straightening up and rolling her shoulders. Her voice was casual, but there was a flicker of curiosity.

Earlier in the week, she'd moved into an RV, which would become her temporary home while he jumped into the demolition part of the job. While he'd been helpful and had assisted in running electricity and sewer out to the trailer, they'd never connected outside the work he was doing at her house.

Jake approached with that easygoing confidence of his, his hands tucked into his pockets. "Thought I'd drop by and let you know we've run into another supply delay. Your kitchen cupboards are backordered, but I put some pressure on the supplier. I work with that company regularly, and they promised to push the order and deliver as early as possible."

Capri sighed, glancing at the half-rebuilt engine in front of her. "I'm used to delays. Things always find a way to go sideways."

He chuckled, leaning casually against the frame of her work truck. "You always expect the worst, don't you?"

She shot him a glance, half a smirk curling on her lips. "I try to be prepared for the unexpected."

Jake nodded, but his gaze lingered on her, like he had something else in mind. "Speaking of unexpected..." He paused as if weighing his next words. "I was thinking, maybe you'd like to take a break from all this and have dinner with me tonight."

Capri blinked, her hand freezing in mid-motion as she wiped the grease from her fingers. She hadn't seen that coming.

"I mean, if you're free," he quickly added. "I was thinking I could cook. I make a mean brisket."

For a split second, she considered brushing him off, making an excuse about being busy. But something in his expression—a mix of sincerity and patience—stopped her.

She surprised herself by saying, "Dinner? Yeah, sure. That sounds...nice."

The words felt foreign on her tongue, and as soon as they were out, she wondered why she hadn't just stuck to her usual distance.

Jake smiled, a slow, genuine curve of his lips that made her stomach do something odd.

"Great," he said, pushing off the truck with a satisfied nod. "Around seven?"

"Yeah," Capri answered, though a wave of uncertainty followed her words. "Seven's fine."

"Great!" He gave her his address and she stored it in her phone

He nodded. "See you tonight."

As Jake walked back to his truck, she stood there, momentarily stunned by her own response. She wasn't the type to say yes to things like this. For years, she had kept everything neatly compartmentalized—her business, her friendships, and especially anything that came close to resembling a romantic entanglement.

She shook her head as if to clear the thought, then turned back to the truck engine. But as she tried to focus on her work, she found her mind drifting, replaying the way Jake had asked her to dinner and the way she hadn't hesitated nearly as long as she normally would have. She hadn't even come up with a reason to say no.

Was it curiosity? Or was it something else?

The wrench in her hand clanged against the metal, pulling her back to reality. "I'm overthinking this," she muttered to herself. "It's just dinner."

But deep down, she wasn't so sure. Dinner with Jake wasn't *just* dinner. He wasn't some random guy from town. He was someone she worked with closely, someone she was starting to see beyond the professional exchanges. She could already feel the shift happening, the subtle ways he looked at her, the way he listened.

And now, she had agreed to dinner.

Capri frowned, her hands stalling as her mind spun with thoughts she'd rather not entertain. She didn't do well with plans or commitments—especially when it came to relationships. There were too many variables, too many things that could fall apart. And yet, she'd said yes.

She stepped back from the engine, wiping her hands clean on an old rag. The knot in her stomach told her that tonight wasn't going to be as simple as dinner and conversation. Jake had expectations, even if he wasn't saying it outright. There was something there, and if she wasn't careful, she'd find herself in deeper than she intended.

Capri blew out a breath, tossing the rag aside. She glanced

at the truck engine and decided it could wait. What she really needed was a long hike to clear her head.

With a quick grab of her bag, she locked up the shop and headed for the trailhead, hoping the solitude of the woods would quiet the nervous fluttering that had settled uncomfortably in her chest. But even as she started the engine of her red pickup, the invitation to dinner lingered, trailing behind her like a shadow she couldn't quite outrun.

23

Capri stood in front of Jake's front door, her hand hovering just inches from the wood. She could hear music faintly playing inside, something bluesy and warm. It struck her as unexpected for a man like Jake—rugged, down-to-earth, with an unpolished edge to him. Taking a deep breath, she knocked twice, wondering for the hundredth time if she should've just said she was too busy.

But the door swung open before she could entertain the thought any longer.

"Hey, glad you made it." Jake greeted her with a warm smile. He was dressed casually, a simple gray Henley that stretched across his broad chest, jeans that looked well-worn from a day of work. His home smelled of roasted garlic and herbs, the kind of scent that felt like comfort wrapped in an embrace.

Capri smiled back, stepping over the threshold. "Yeah, well, figured I should probably eat something that wasn't takeout for a change." She tried to sound light, but there was a nervousness in her voice, a tension she couldn't quite shake.

He led her through a living room that was decorated simply

—leather furnishings and uncluttered wood tables—and into the kitchen where a small dining table was set for two. It was cozy and intimate, the dim lighting from above casting a soft glow over the plates.

Once again, Capri considered this might be more than a simple invite to dinner. She quickly pushed the thought aside.

"This looks amazing," she said, her eyes falling on the roasted brisket, green beans, and mashed potatoes spread across the table. It was hearty, comforting—just like the smell of the house.

Jake chuckled. "Don't be too impressed. It's a family recipe, but I've made it enough times not to mess it up."

As they sat down, the clinking of utensils filled the silence. Capri was hyper-aware of everything—the closeness of the table, the way Jake's eyes lingered on her a little longer than she was used to. She filled her plate, hoping to keep the conversation neutral.

"So," Jake began, after a few bites, "I was thinking...we should take a trip next weekend. There's this little shop here in Jackson I've been meaning to show you. They've got great ideas for outdoor furniture, maybe something we could use to spruce up your porch."

Capri swallowed, the bite of brisket suddenly feeling heavy in her throat. She nodded, though she didn't meet his eyes. "Yeah, sounds nice."

Jake leaned back in his chair, studying her. "Or, you know, there's this trail up in the Tetons I haven't hiked in a while. Thought it might be fun to do it together. What do you think?"

And there it was—that shift she'd been waiting for. Fun things to do together. Projects. Plans. She could feel the expectations rising, like a wave pushing her toward something she wasn't ready to face.

Capri set down her fork and glanced around the room, her fingers brushing the edge of the napkin in her lap. "That sounds great, Jake, but...I've got a lot going on with the rafting company. I'm not sure I have time to think about hiking or outdoor furniture right now."

Jake raised an eyebrow. "Sure, I get that. But we all need a break sometimes, don't we?"

His question felt too pointed, too...personal. Capri shifted in her seat, a small knot forming in her stomach. She needed to steer this back into safer territory—work.

"Speaking of breaks, how's the timeline looking for the house? I've been thinking about the fixtures. I believe I finally decided which ones I want to go with."

Jake tilted his head, his easygoing smile slipping just a little. "We're on schedule, don't worry about that. But I wasn't talking about work."

Capri could feel the weight of his words, and it made her uneasy. She wanted to keep things professional, controlled. Jake wasn't supposed to cross that line, wasn't supposed to start hinting at... more.

Jake let the silence settle between them for a moment before he leaned forward, his voice gentler now. "You seem uncomfortable, Capri. Every time we talk about something that's not work, it's like you're pulling back. Is there a reason for that?"

Her heart raced as she forced herself to meet his eyes. The sincerity in his gaze made her stomach flip. She hated this—hated feeling like she was losing control of the conversation, of the situation.

"I'm not pulling back," she lied, her voice steadier than she felt. "I just...don't do well with plans or commitments. Never have."

Jake didn't say anything right away. His blue eyes searched her face as if he was trying to see past the mask she always wore. "I wasn't asking for a commitment," he said slowly, "just a little time. But if that's more than you're ready for, I understand."

Capri forced a smile, reaching for her glass of water as a way to break the tension. "It's not that, Jake. I just need to keep my focus right now. The renovation, the rafting business, all of it. I don't have room for...any distraction."

The word hung between them, more loaded than she intended. Jake didn't flinch, though. He nodded, his expression thoughtful. "Alright. I won't push. Just know I really like you. I'd like to be friends...maybe explore where that takes us."

She nodded, feeling relief and guilt all at once. His patience gave her space to breathe, to figure out her own tangled emotions without the pressure of expectation. It wasn't that she didn't like him—if anything, his presence was starting to feel like the one solid thing in her life. But for now, she needed time, and Jake seemed to understand that perfectly.

As they finished dinner, the conversation drifted back to safer topics—work, the house, the town. But the words Jake had said stayed with her, lingering long after she left his house that evening.

She told herself this was just about protection, keeping things in check. But as she drove home, a nagging thought crept in. What if she was pushing away something good—something real—because she didn't know how to let someone in?

24

Over the next few weeks, Capri settled into an easy rhythm with Jake. The initial push-pull between them had softened, replaced by a subtle understanding. They worked well together, despite her instinct to keep him at arm's length.

Jake had a way of diffusing tension with a calm, dependable approach that allowed them to make solid progress on the renovations. Bit by bit, the old house transformed under their hands—walls were knocked down, floors replaced, the fresh scent of sawdust and new beginnings filling the air.

Capri still felt the occasional flicker of hesitation, that familiar need to pull back when things felt too close, but the work kept them focused. Each day, they found more common ground, though she remained cautious about where it all might lead.

Still, she was learning to trust Jake. He showed up every day on time, worked diligently, and as promised, leaving her to focus on the rafting company and the arduous tourist season. More than once, she returned home exhausted, only to find him packing up with a glass of iced tea waiting for her.

Today had been particularly trying. A family of five had booked the afternoon raft tour, and from the moment they arrived, Capri's nerves were on edge.

The parents seemed blissfully unaware as their three young children tore through the equipment area like miniature tornados, grabbing at paddles and life vests, knocking over supplies, and shrieking at the top of their lungs.

Capri's jaw clenched as she tried to maintain her usual professional demeanor, though inside she was fuming. The youngest boy had already fallen into the shallow water twice before they even boarded, and the older two were locked in a constant state of sibling warfare, shoving and arguing while their mother distractedly scrolled through her phone.

Capri loved running her rafting business, but days like this —days when parents seemed to treat her tours like a daycare— made her question her life choices. By the time they finally launched, her temples throbbed with the beginnings of a headache, and she had to remind herself to breathe as the kids banged around the raft, completely oblivious to her instructions.

The draining experience had left her with a slight headache.

When the ordeal was finally over, Capri returned home and walked up to her cabin, her boots kicking up dust from the well-trodden path. The day had been long. Not only with the family from hell, but full of small setbacks and endless meetings. All she wanted now was a hot shower and a moment to breathe before tackling the next set of decisions for the house renovation.

But as soon as she turned the corner to her porch, her steps faltered.

There, set up neatly on the front porch, was a brand-new set of outdoor furniture—two rustic wooden chairs with deep cushions and a small table between them. The kind of furniture that would've looked perfect in a catalog but now felt glaringly out of place. Her heart thudded in her chest.

She dropped her bag on the ground, her hands going to her hips as she stared at the chairs. It didn't take long to put the pieces together.

Jake.

Just as she was about to storm inside, the screen door swung open, and there he was, wiping his hands on a rag like he had no idea the world was about to explode. He glanced at the furniture, then at her, his easy smile in place. "Hey, you're back earlier than I thought. I finished up some work inside and figured I'd surprise you."

Capri felt her irritation bubbling up, her hands clenching into fists. "Surprise me? With this?" She gestured to the furniture like it was something offensive. "Jake, what were you thinking?"

His smile faded, replaced with confusion. "What do you mean? You said you wanted something cozy for the porch. I found this set at a good price, thought it fit the space. Just trying to help."

Her pulse quickened. *Help.* That word, so innocent, sent her spiraling. She had asked for cozy, yes, but this wasn't about the chairs. It was about control—about decisions being made without her.

"You should have asked me first," she snapped, crossing her arms over her chest. "This is my house, Jake. Every decision, big or small, needs to go through me. I thought we were clear on that."

Jake frowned, stepping toward her but keeping his distance. "I didn't think it was that big of a deal. You've got a million things going on—I figured this would be one less thing to worry about."

"That's not the point!" Capri's voice rose, frustration pushing her words out faster than she could control them. "You can't just go around making decisions for me. I need to be involved in every detail. I need to know what's happening, what's being bought, what's being changed."

Jake's face softened, though his eyes held a flicker of frustration. "Capri, I'm not trying to take control of anything. I'm just trying to make things easier for you. This was supposed to be a gesture, not a problem."

But it was a problem. Everything felt like a problem when she wasn't in control. "You don't get it," she muttered, shaking her head. "If I don't stay on top of things, they fall apart. That's just how it is."

Jake took a deep breath, his voice calm but firm. "I get that you like to have things done your way, but Capri, sometimes people can help without it being a bad thing. This isn't about taking control from you. It's about making things better—for you."

Capri stared at him, her heartbeat loud in her ears. She knew, deep down, that he was right. That he wasn't trying to undermine her. But she couldn't let go of the gnawing fear that if she stopped paying attention to every detail, something would slip away, unraveling everything she'd worked so hard to hold together.

Her voice wavered. "You don't understand. I can't just... let things go. It doesn't work like that."

Then it started.

Her heart raced uncontrollably, thudding against her ribcage like it was trying to escape. Cold sweat trickled down her spine, and a terrifying sense of doom gripped her, overwhelming her thoughts with a flood of fear she couldn't name or control. She reached for Jake, gasping, trying to ground herself in a reality that was slipping away.

Concern immediately sprouted on his face. "Capri? Are you alright?"

He led her to one of the new chairs and gently pushed her

to sit. "You look like you're going to faint." He squatted beside her, took her hands in his, and squeezed. "Take a deep breath."

She did as she was told, fought to gain control by squeezing her eyes tightly shut.

Breathe in...breathe out.

What seemed like an eternity passed before her heart quit racing. Trembling, she wiped the sheen of sweat from her forehead and swallowed.

Jake stood. "Stay here. I'm getting you a glass of water."

He headed inside and was back in seconds, thrusting the glass to her lips. "Take a drink."

She placed her hand on his, thankful for his care and concern. She took a sip, then a longer one. "Thanks, I'm okay now," she told him, hoping that was true.

They sat in silence for several minutes. He let go of one of her hands and rubbed her arm with little circles. Letting down her defenses, she let herself lean into him. He felt...safe.

Finally, he broke the silence. "Do you do that often?" he asked, brushing a damp strand of her hair off her face.

"What?" she asked weakly.

"The panic thing."

Filled with shame, she quietly shook her head. "No. Just a couple of times. It only happens when..." She let her words drift.

"When your feelings get too big?"

She gazed up at him, fighting back tears of shame, and simply nodded.

Jake's expression softened even more, his patience unwavering. "I think you're afraid of something bigger than porch furniture, Capri."

Her throat tightened at the truth in his words. She wanted to deny it, but she couldn't. Not really. "I just need to know what's going on," she whispered, more to herself than to him.

She cautiously removed her other hand from his.

Jake nodded slowly, respecting the space she was creating between them, even if he didn't like it. "I get that. But you don't have to shoulder everything all alone. That's what I'm trying to say."

Capri clenched her jaw, swallowing the lump of guilt rising in her chest. She wanted to apologize, to tell him she had been unreasonable. But the fear still clung to her, making her feel like if she gave an inch, everything could slip out of her grasp.

Instead, she crossed her arms over her chest. "Just... next time, run it by me, okay?"

Jake met her eyes, his gaze unwavering. "Okay," he said softly, but there was a hint of disappointment in his voice. He stood, and after confirming she was feeling better, he turned back toward the door. "I'll be inside if you need anything."

As the door closed behind him, Capri let out a long breath, her shoulders sagging. The sight of the new furniture, so thoughtfully placed, now felt heavy with the weight of her own stubbornness.

She glanced at the chairs again, the simple beauty of them mocking her resistance. Jake had only been trying to help, and she had turned it into a battleground over something deeper than either of them could name.

Capri sighed, rubbing her hands over her face, the guilt settling in. She knew she was wrong. But admitting that to herself was one thing. Letting go of the control she clung to so fiercely?

That was something else entirely.

25

The late afternoon sun sank toward the horizon, stretching long shadows across the yard. Capri stood near the open garage, the scent of freshly cut wood mingling with the crisp mountain air. Pine and sagebrush teased her senses, but the faint smell of sawdust and varnish brought her back to the task at hand.

Jake had the radio playing softly in the background—a country song she didn't recognize—and the rhythmic sound of his hammer striking nails blended with the breeze rustling the leaves of the nearby aspens.

The cabin renovations were moving along, but Capri couldn't shake the unease that clung to her ever since Jake had shown up with the patio furniture—sturdy and timeless, made of dark, weathered wood with thick, hand-carved details that spoke of craftsmanship.

Jake meant it as a thoughtful gesture. But to Capri, it felt like a loss of control—a symbol of the small but growing divide between what she wanted and what he was offering. She'd overreacted and thrown herself into another panic episode. Worse? He'd witnessed it.

Her hand tightened around the measuring tape, the sharp bite of the metal immediately causing her to pull back. "Ouch!"

Her outburst caught Jake's attention. "You okay?"

"Yeah." She shook her head as she sucked on the tiny cut on her thumb. "Just careless." She measured the next plank.

Capri forced herself to focus, cutting lengths of wood for the beams, but her hands trembled as she reached for the saw.

Being around Jake unsettled Capri in ways she hadn't expected. His calm, unruffled nature was like a quiet current she couldn't escape. There was a confidence in the way he carried himself, his deep voice unhurried, never rattled, which both grounded her and made her want to pull away. But it was more than just his demeanor. There was something about the way he moved, the way his broad shoulders filled out a simple flannel shirt, or how his hands—strong, capable, and deliberate—caught her attention, especially the ease with which he handled things, whether it was a hammer or a bundle of wood.

The faint scruff along his jaw, the hint of muscles under his work-worn clothes, and the way his eyes softened when he looked at her made her pulse quicken. She was drawn to him, no question about it, but that pull terrified her as much as it thrilled her.

Even now, she could feel his gaze on her, lingering more often than not. It was a wonder he got anything done with how many times he kept looking her way.

Capri felt a flicker of warmth beneath her unease, a mixture of flattery and frustration. Part of her wanted to meet his gaze, to acknowledge the attention, but she focused on the task at hand, unwilling to let down her guard.

Capri realized she needed a carpenter's square to make sure her cuts were precise. Glancing around, she couldn't find it among the scattered tools. Her eyes settled on Dick's old toolbox, perched on a high shelf in the garage. With a small sigh, she reached for it, feeling the familiar weight of the weathered metal. When she opened the lid, her breath caught. Lying there, nestled among the worn tools, was a small toy stick horse Dick had carved for her when she was young. Its wood was smooth and simple, the kind of thing only a child would treasure. Tears pricked at her eyes as the memories came rushing back.

Jake noticed her pause and stepped closer, setting down his measuring tape. "Everything alright?" he asked, his voice soft as he nodded toward the toy horse.

Capri blinked, trying to steady herself. "Dick made this for me when I was little," she said quietly, her fingers grazing the polished wood. "Back before...before things started to fall apart."

There was a long pause.

"Let's take a break," Jake suggested, motioning out the garage door.

She reluctantly nodded and followed him outside and up the steps to the porch where a pitcher of tea waited beside two empty glasses. He took the liberty of pouring and handed her the drink.

As she sank into one of the patio chairs, a tiny smile nipped at the corners of her mouth. "These are pretty nice cushions," she admitted.

Her comment brought an amused look into Jake's eyes. "I told you I'm happy to return them."

"Nah, I decided to keep the set. The furniture is growing on me." She diverted her gaze. That wasn't all that was growing on her.

Jake leaned back against his chair. He glanced over to the sawhorse just inside the open garage, eyeing the wood Capri was measuring. "That beam's a little long, don't you think?" he said, half-smiling.

Capri rolled her eyes playfully. "I know what I'm doing,

thank you very much. I'm no novice to building things. Dick taught me a lot."

Jake continued to grin. "Fair enough, but just saying, precision matters. Even on a Saturday."

She raised an eyebrow. "Speaking of Saturday, shouldn't you be out enjoying it? Most people don't spend their weekends covered in sawdust. I'm a tough boss, but I'm not known for working people 'round the clock."

Jake shrugged, giving her a sideways glance. "Could say the same about you. I thought you'd be trekking up some mountain trail, not cooped up here helping me fix up an old cabin."

Capri smiled slightly. "Trust me, I considered it. But this place needs work, and I like seeing progress. Plus, I'm not exactly the sit-around type."

Jake grinned. "Yeah, I've noticed."

There was another brief silence before he continued. "I also noticed you teared up when you spotted the toy horse. Wanna talk about it?"

Capri stiffened slightly, her fingers tightening around the glass she was holding. She hadn't expected him to bring the subject up, and for a moment, she considered brushing it off. But the way Jake asked—calm, without pressing—made her hesitate. She set the glass down and glanced into the open garage door, over at the toolbox where the little toy horse still sat.

"It's just a reminder," she said quietly, her voice measured. "Of when things were less complicated. Dick used to make me things like that when I was a kid. Before...well, before he started drinking."

She paused, feeling the familiar knot tighten in her chest, unsure if she wanted to continue—unsure she wanted to talk about any of this with Jake.

"I'd like to hear about it," he prompted. "Dick sounds like he was quite a guy."

"He was," Capri quickly answered. "He married my mom when I was still fairly young. He was the only dad I ever knew, and, except for the years he was drinking, he treated me like a daughter." She paused. "I loved him very much."

Wanting to divert the attention off herself, she directed her gaze at Jake. "What about you?"

"What do you mean?"

"C'mon—spill. You mentioned you grew up in Alabama. What was your childhood like?"

Jake leaned back in his chair, his fingers resting around his glass as he thought for a moment. His expression softened, a faint smile tugging at the corner of his lips.

"Well," he began, "I grew up in a small town in northern Alabama. Not too different from Thunder Mountain in some ways. Tight-knit community, everyone knew each other's business. My parents had a farm—nothing big, but we grew a little of everything. We sold at local farmers' markets. It was a simple life."

He paused, and his gaze grew distant as if he were looking back through time. "I was the youngest of five kids, so I had my fair share of fights and competition growing up. My two brothers were always bigger, stronger. I had to work twice as hard just to keep up. My dad—well, he wasn't easy. Stubborn as a mule. He had a way of making you feel like no matter what you did, it wasn't enough." Jake's smile faded.

Capri shifted slightly, noticing a flicker of tension cross his face. "Sounds tough."

"Yeah," he said quietly. "It was. But it taught me something valuable—how to rely on myself. My brothers left early, went off to do their own things. I stayed on the farm longer, helped my mom after Dad passed. Eventually, she made the decision to sell. But...I knew I wasn't meant to be there forever. I always had this feeling I was supposed to build something of my own."

Capri nodded, her eyes softening. "And that brought you here?"

"Eventually, yeah. I went to school, got into architecture, and that's when things started to make sense. I loved the idea of creating something lasting, something people could live in and feel safe. After a few years of working all over, I ended up in Jackson Hole, fell in love with the mountains. It's hard to explain, but once I was here, it felt like home in a way Alabama never did."

Capri felt a strange pull in her chest as Jake spoke, his words weaving together pieces of his life that she hadn't known before. She could hear the pride in his voice, but there was something else—something deeper. Maybe a touch of loneliness that mirrored her own.

He shrugged as if brushing off the heaviness of the moment. "So yeah, that's me. Not much to tell."

Capri's lips twitched into a half-smile. "I think there's a lot more to you than you're letting on."

Jake chuckled, a deep, warm sound that made Capri's heart skip. "Maybe," he said, meeting her gaze. "But I figure some things are better learned with time, don't you?"

Before she could reply, Capri felt a flutter in her stomach, the familiar unease creeping in. His words hung between them, filled with a promise she wasn't sure she was ready to accept.

What happens next could go two ways—Capri could deflect again, pushing away the growing connection between them by changing the subject or pulling back emotionally. Or, for the first time, she might let the conversation linger, acknowledging the potential of something more with Jake.

She hesitated; a question lodged in her throat. After a moment of grappling with herself, Capri lifted her gaze to meet his. "Have you ever been in love?"

Jake's eyebrows shot up, clearly taken aback. "Whoa, I wasn't expecting that." Despite his initial surprise, a smile tugged at his lips, and he let out a soft laugh. "Yeah...yeah, I have."

He waited for her response, but Capri gave him a sly look, shaking her head. "Oh no, I asked you first."

Jake's smile softened as he ran a hand through his hair as if the memory lingered just beneath the surface. "Her name was Sophie. We met in college—she was studying journalism. She had this fire in her, always chasing the next big story, dreaming of traveling the world and covering things that mattered."

He paused, his eyes flicking to Capri's, then down to his hands. "It was easy between us, you know? Real. But... in the end, we wanted different things."

Capri raised an eyebrow. "What happened?"

Jake let out a quiet sigh. "She wanted to see the world, report from places like war zones, uncovering truths that people needed to hear. And I—I wanted something simpler. A place to call home, a life I could build with my own hands. We sat down one day and realized neither of us could give up what we wanted for the other. No blowout fight or angry words...just a simple understanding that we were headed in different directions."

He shrugged, trying to mask the lingering hurt with a casual gesture. "It made sense, practical even. But that didn't stop it from cutting deep when it ended."

Capri felt the gravity of his words settle between them. That was something she wasn't sure she'd ever had. The way Jake spoke about Sophie, so matter of fact yet laced with unspoken heartache, made her stomach twist.

She'd always believed love was something she could keep at a distance, something that couldn't touch her if she didn't let it. But sitting here, listening to Jake talk about what he had lost for the sake of practicality, made her realize how foreign that kind of connection was to her.

Jake watched her for a moment, reading the silence in her

expression. "Your turn," he said gently, nudging her with his words. "What about you? Ever been in love?"

Capri swallowed, feeling exposed under his steady gaze. But no doubt she'd asked for it.

She shifted in her seat, almost wishing she could brush off the question.

"No," she said quietly, admitting it to herself for the first time. "I've never been in love. Not really."

The words felt heavier than she expected, like she was confessing something more than just a fact—something deeper about the way she'd lived her life, always keeping people at arm's length.

Jake held her gaze, his expression softening with understanding. "There's no rush, you know," he said, his voice low and reassuring. "Love comes when it's meant to, not when we try to force it."

Capri gave him a small, wistful smile, feeling the truth of his words settle into the space between them. "Maybe," she murmured. "But I'm not sure I'd even know what to do if it did."

26

Reva sat back in her office chair, staring at the email that glared back at her from the computer screen. The subject line alone was enough to make her want to close the laptop and pretend it didn't exist.

URGENT: Seismic Safety Mandate for Thunder Mountain Public Buildings.

The office around her was quiet, save for the faint hum of the air conditioner. The renovation had done wonders to erase the water damage from the flood earlier in the year, but now it felt like she had barely enjoyed the space before another disaster landed on her desk.

The walls were painted a soft sage, the new flooring solid beneath her feet, and yet everything felt off-kilter—like the ground beneath her feet could shift again at any moment. And it had been. Tremors had been shaking Thunder Mountain for weeks now, but this email made it clear things were about to get worse. At least for her and the municipality of Thunder Mountain.

She looked at the colorful drawing Lucan had given her a few days ago, taped to the edge of her monitor. His simple crayon strokes were a bright reminder of everything she was trying to protect, but even that small comfort couldn't distract her from the reality spelled out in neat, cold text in the email.

The U.S. Geological Survey and FEMA were mandating seismic upgrades for all public buildings in Thunder Mountain. They needed to meet stricter safety codes immediately or face fines—and worse, the possible closure of critical facilities that the town relied on. Even the small, cherished library and the new community center, a popular gathering spot, weren't exempt from the new requirements.

The costs? Astronomical. The town's budget couldn't stretch that far, not even close. The government offered loans, of course, but those came with strings that could pull Thunder Mountain into financial ruin for years.

The urgency of these upgrades weighed heavily. Resources were already stretched thin.

Reva let out a long sigh, pushing her hair back from her face as she stood and moved to the window. Outside, the trees lining Main Street were beginning to turn a deeper shade of green as summer settled in. The peaceful scene outside her office window did nothing to calm her mind. The weight of it all sat heavy on her chest.

How was she supposed to explain this to the town? The people who could barely afford their own homes, let alone pay extra assessments for retrofitting old buildings that had withstood decades without incident.

The office door swung open suddenly, and Reva startled, her hand flying to her chest.

Capri stood in the doorway, one hand gripping the handle, her face flushed as if she'd rushed over. She wore her usual outdoor gear—jeans, a fitted fleece jacket, and hiking boots, dirt smeared on her knees, looking like she had just come back from the river. "Sorry, didn't mean to scare you," she said, closing the door behind her. "You weren't answering your phone, so I decided to drop by."

Reva exhaled, trying to settle her racing heart. "No, it's fine. I just—" She gestured vaguely to the screen. "Got some... news."

Capri raised an eyebrow and sauntered over, glancing at the screen as she flopped down in the chair across from Reva's desk. "FEMA? What, are we getting disaster funds? I thought the earthquake damage wasn't that bad."

Reva shook her head and sat down, feeling the tension start to creep into her shoulders. "No, not exactly. They're imposing strict new regulations on all the public buildings in town. The school, city hall, the community center—all of them need to be retrofitted to meet updated seismic codes. And it's going to cost... well, way more than we have."

Capri's face shifted from curiosity to a frown, her brow furrowing as she processed the information. "What? You're kidding. We've felt a few tremors, but nothing serious. Even the expert you brought in reassured us that this kind of thing is rare around here."

"That's not how the government sees it," Reva muttered, leaning back in her chair. "They want us to be prepared for 'worst-case scenarios,' which is understandable...but we don't have the money. Not without getting into serious debt. And I don't know how the town's going to react when they find out."

"Can't you fight it?" Capri asked.

Reva shook her head. "We could. But attorney fees would be costly, even if I did most of the legal work. In the end, we're not likely to prevail. Public safety often trumps everything else when you take these things to court."

Capri crossed her arms, leaning back in her seat, clearly irritated. "So, what? We're just supposed to fork out money we don't have because some suit in Washington says we might have a bigger earthquake?"

Reva nodded grimly. "Exactly. And if we don't comply, they'll shut down the buildings. Can you imagine the school closing or the chapel? The town would fall apart."

Capri was silent for a moment, staring at the ceiling as if trying to wrestle down her frustration. "You've got to be kidding me. This is the last thing we need right now. Tell them we're not Los Angeles or Dallas—Thunder Mountain doesn't have that kind of money lying around."

"I know, Capri. Believe me, I am fully aware of the issue," Reva said, rubbing her temples. "But it doesn't matter. The mandate is nonnegotiable. We either comply, or face fines. Worse, we lose the town's resources."

Capri blew out a breath and stood, pacing the small office. "What's the plan, then? You can't just break this news at the next town meeting and hope for the best. People are going to freak out. You need a strategy."

Reva watched her friend pace, the fire in Capri's eyes a stark contrast to how overwhelmed she felt. "True, but I just got the news. Perhaps we could organize some kind of fundraiser, get the community involved. The Knit Wit ladies will probably try to help with something...but fundraising isn't going to begin to cover what we need."

Capri paused mid-step, her eyes narrowing in thought. "Maybe. But you've got to go bigger. You need to get people fired up. Make it about saving the town, not just paying for upgrades. We'll have to do this online and get the word out far and wide."

Reva bit her lip, mulling over Capri's words. "I like how you are thinking. Unlike Jackson and other nearby towns, we'll have to drum up financial support. I'm nearly certain people would rally around helping."

Capri turned, hands on her hips, her gaze sharp. "They have to. This town means too much to everyone to let it fall apart because of some out-of-touch government mandate. You make it personal, make it about the future. We'll figure it out. Heavens, I'll talk to Bodhi, maybe we can organize something at Grand Teton Whitewater—urge some tourists to pitch in. People like a good cause."

Reva's shoulders relaxed just a little as Capri's words sank in. She had been so focused on the overwhelming cost and logistics that she hadn't considered what her friends—and the community—could really accomplish when they pulled together.

"Okay," Reva said, a small smile creeping onto her face. "You're right. We'll figure this out. Maybe it's not impossible after all."

Capri gave her a determined nod. "Dang right, it's not. We've gotten through worse than this."

Reva couldn't help but feel a flicker of hope. They might be facing another storm, but maybe, just maybe, they could weather this one too.

"I think you're onto something," she admitted to Capri. She stood, came around the desk, and gave her friend a quick hug. "But that doesn't answer why you stormed into my office. What's up?"

Capri immediately sank into Reva's office chair and plopped her head into her hands. "I'm in trouble."

Alarm caused Reva to stiffen. "Oh, honey. What's the matter?"

"I'm falling for him."

"For whom?"

Capri looked up; her face painted with misery. "Jake Carrington."

Reva couldn't help herself. She threw her head back and laughed. "And that's a problem? Why?"

Tears sprouted in her friend's eyes. "Because."

Capri glanced down at her hands, twisting them nervously. "I didn't expect this, Reva. Falling for Jake—it scares the heck out of me. I'm not good at this...at letting someone in. Every time he tries to get closer, I feel like I'm standing on the edge of something, and I don't know if I'll fall or fly. What if I mess it up? What if he sees all my flaws and runs? Or worse—what if he doesn't run, and I'm the one who can't handle it? I don't know how to let go without losing control. I think I'm broken."

Reva shook her head. "What? You think you need to do this perfectly? With no flaws, no missteps?" She bent before her friend and clasped her hands into her own, her gaze directed at Capri's face. "Remember when my relationship with Merritt Hardwick fell apart?"

Capri nodded. "Yeah, I remember. You were a wreck for months."

Reva felt her expression soften. "Yes, I was. And I soothed my hurting heart by numbing it with alcohol. I got myself in a world of trouble."

Capri wiped her nose with the back of her hand. "Yeah. So, what has that got to do with my situation?"

A slight smile nipped at the corners of Reva's lips. "Let me share a profound lesson I learned when I had reached my breaking point. I was cooking one night, crying my eyes out, and thinking about my life and how everything felt fractured." She let her smile grow a little wider. "I began to make corn-bread and cracked these two eggs and suddenly, as if God was standing right before me, I heard him say, 'Now I can use you!'"

She paused. "You see, an egg can't be used until it's broken."

27

C apri stood on her porch, phone in hand, her thumb trembling as it hovered over the "send" button. The text she'd typed was simple. *Would you want to go for a ride? I was thinking Charlie Grace's ranch tomorrow.* Yet, the invitation it carried felt monumental. Her heart raced, a tangle of nerves and excitement twisting inside her. After everything with Jake, every step forward felt precarious. One wrong move, and she feared things might spiral out of control, moving too fast for her to handle.

She stared at the message, reading and rereading it. Was it too casual? Did it sound like she didn't care enough? Or maybe it sounded like she cared too much? She shook her head, chastising herself for overthinking. Reva's voice echoed in her mind, reminding her to be okay with not having it all figured out.

With a deep breath, Capri hit send and immediately regretted it. Her pulse quickened as she waited for his response, a cocktail of anticipation and fear bubbling beneath the surface.

Her phone buzzed, making her jump.

Sounds perfect. What time?

His quick reply both thrilled and unnerved her. She hadn't expected him to be so eager, but that was Jake—unwavering, patient, and seemingly unfazed by her hesitations. Capri set the time and put her phone down, exhaling the breath she hadn't realized she was holding. She had taken the first step. It wasn't a leap, but it was something.

The next day, Capri arrived at Charlie Grace's guest ranch earlier than planned. She told herself it was to help saddle the horses, but deep down, she knew it was because of her nerves.

She stepped from her truck and looked around at the wide-open space filled with treetops colliding with blue sky. The fresh air felt so expansive, or so full of possibilities—making her feel both alive and utterly exposed.

Charlie Grace appeared at the barn door and waved. "Hey! I didn't expect you until later."

"Sorry," Capri said, a little breathless as she approached. "I got ready quicker than I thought. Guess I just couldn't sit still, so here I am." She gave a small, nervous laugh, hoping it didn't sound as shaky as she felt.

Charlie Grace gave her a knowing smile, but to her credit, she didn't ask questions. "The horses are ready," she said, leading her to two sturdy geldings. "You picked a beautiful day for a ride. I'll leave you to it."

"Are you sure this is no trouble?" Capri asked.

"Not an issue in the slightest. We have no guest excursions planned for today, so take your time." Her friend winked, struggling to conceal her delight at the prospect of Capri and Jake being together.

Ignoring Charlie Grace's enthusiasm, Capri stroked the horse's neck, her fingers tracing the familiar lines of muscle and hair, using the routine as a way to calm her thoughts. When she heard Jake's truck pull up, her heart did a little flip, and she took another steadying breath. She could do this.

Jake strolled toward her, looking like he'd just stepped out of an ad for rugged outdoor gear—boots dusted with dirt, worn jeans that fit just right, and a button-down shirt with the sleeves rolled up, revealing strong forearms. His hair was windswept, his face kissed by the sun. The sight of him made her pulse quicken, and Capri cursed herself for how easily he affected her.

"Hey," Jake greeted her, that familiar smile softening his sharp features. He reached for her hand, just briefly, but it was enough to make her skin tingle. "Thanks for the invite."

"Yeah, sure," Capri replied, keeping her tone casual, though inside she was anything but. "I figured a ride would be more fun than...you know, working on the house."

He chuckled, his eyes twinkling as he glanced at the horses. "Can't argue with that."

She didn't add that she'd considered asking him to dinner at her favorite restaurant in Jackson—the White Buffalo Club. A second dinner date, especially in such a romantic setting, felt too intimate, too formal.

They mounted their horses in comfortable silence, and soon they were on the trail, the rhythmic clip-clop of hooves the only sound at first. The trail wove through the open meadow and into the wooded hills, where the scent of pine and sagebrush filled the air. Capri felt a little calmer now, her body falling into the familiar rhythm of riding. But every now and then, she'd catch Jake's gaze flicking toward her, and her stomach would do a somersault.

As they rode, conversation came easily.

Capri toyed with the reins, glancing at Jake. "So, what's your guilty pleasure? How do you like to fill your free time?" she asked with a smile, hoping to keep the conversation light.

Jake chuckled softly, rubbing his chin as he thought. "Okay, don't judge me, but I've got a serious thing for reality cooking shows."

Capri raised an eyebrow, surprised. "Seriously? Like the competitive ones?"

"Yep," he grinned. "There's something about the intensity, the chaos in the kitchen, and how they whip up something amazing from nothing. Plus, I can't cook to save my life, so I guess I live vicariously."

Capri laughed, the sound easy. "You? That's not true. The brisket you prepared was delicious."

"I'm not a real cook," Jake admitted. "I can grill a decent steak or fix a recipe or two my mom shared with me, but anything more complicated than that, and it's a disaster."

"Well, good thing you're handy with construction and renovations," Capri teased, feeling her tension ease even further.

Jake shot her a playful look. "What about you? What's something no one would guess about you?"

Capri paused, thinking for a moment. "Well, in addition to my *Gilmore Girls* addiction, I have a ridiculous obsession with old murder mysteries—Agatha Christie, Sherlock Holmes, that sort of thing. I can spend hours curled up with one of those books or binging the old TV adaptations."

"Didn't peg you for the mystery type," Jake said, surprised. "Do you solve the cases before they reveal the culprit?"

"Sometimes," she replied, grinning. "But half the fun is trying to piece it all together. I especially adore a couple of new mystery authors I've stumbled upon—Jana DeLeon and Tonya Kappes."

As they continued down the trail, the conversation meandered into unexpected territory—favorite childhood memories, secret ambitions, and the quirks that made them who they were. Capri found herself laughing more than she had in a while, and with each passing moment, she realized how easy it felt to be with Jake, even if the undercurrent of fear still lingered. But for now, she pushed apprehension aside, allowing herself to enjoy the ride and the company.

Their legs brushed occasionally as the trail narrowed, and every time, a jolt of awareness shot through Capri. Once, as Jake reached to adjust his saddlebag, his hand grazed hers, and the simple touch sent a thrill up her spine. Each brush of skin, each subtle connection, felt charged, and it was becoming harder to ignore the pull between them.

After a while, they reached a quiet clearing. The vista stretched out before them; a valley spread wide beneath the towering peaks. Capri dismounted first, her legs stiff but her heart beating with anticipation. Jake followed suit, walking over to where she stood by a large rock. He stood close and when she turned to look at him, her breath caught at the way his eyes lingered on her face.

"This is beautiful," he said, but his gaze never left hers.

"It is," she agreed, though she wasn't sure if he was talking about the view anymore.

For a long moment, neither of them spoke. The air between them was thick with unspoken tension, and Capri could feel her heart now racing—the magnetic pull drawing her closer to him, inch by inch. Before she could stop herself, she reached up to brush a strand of hair behind her ear, and in that moment, Jake stepped forward. His hand gently cupped her face, his thumb grazing her cheek.

"Capri..." he murmured, his voice low and full of something that sent a shiver through her.

And then, he kissed her.

The world seemed to still in that moment, the wind holding its breath, the trees standing silent witness. His lips were soft but sure, and the kiss was slow, tender, like he was savoring every second. Capri's breath caught as she leaned into him, her hand instinctively finding its way to his chest. The heat of him, the solidness of him, was both overwhelming and comforting all at once. A rush of warmth flooded her chest, spreading through her, making her forget, for a moment, all the reasons she had to be afraid.

But as much as she wanted to stay in that moment, the familiar panic began to creep in. The kiss deepened, and with it came the realization of just how fast this was all happening. She wasn't ready. Not yet. Not for this.

Capri pulled away, breathless and shaken, her heart hammering in her chest. "Jake, I..." Her voice faltered as the words tangled in her throat.

Jake stepped back immediately, his hand falling away, though his eyes stayed locked on hers. He looked concerned but not surprised, as if he knew this might happen. "It's okay," he said softly. "We don't have to rush anything."

Her chest ached with the weight of her own fear. She wanted this—wanted him—but the fear of what it all meant, of what it could lead to, was suffocating. She could do casual relationships that were meant to lead nowhere—but this?

"I just..." She shook her head, frustrated at her inability to explain the turmoil inside.

Jake's expression remained calm, and his eyes held hers with quiet understanding. He didn't push, didn't question her hesitation, just let the moment settle between them. After a beat, he spoke, his voice soft and steady.

"Capri," he began, his tone gentle but firm, "I get that you're scared. Life throws a lot at us, and sometimes it feels like we have to handle it all on our own. But no one's meant to go through this stuff alone. When hard times hit, that's when we need each other the most."

He took her shoulders and turned her toward the clearing. "See those sunflowers?"

She nodded, wondering where he was going with this.

"Sunflowers turn according to the position of the sun. In other words, they chase the light." He squeezed her hand. "You might already know this, but there is another fact you probably do not know."

Jake bent and plucked a bloom from its tall stem. "Have you ever wondered what happens on cloudy and rainy days when the sun is completely covered by clouds? You'd think the sunflower withers or turns its head towards the ground. You'd be wrong."

He tucked the bloom into her hand. "Instead, they turn towards each other to share their energy. Nature's perfection is amazing. And, it has so much to teach us...don't you think?"

He paused, searching her face as if trying to reach the part of her that was still walled off. "I'm not saying everything gets fixed just by being with someone. Yet, when you've got a special person by your side, it makes the weight of things a little lighter. We're all a little scared, Capri. But we don't have to be scared alone."

He took a step closer, his hand brushing hers lightly, offering connection without pressure. "I'm not asking for anything you're not ready for. But don't shut me out because you're afraid of what could go wrong. Let me in—just a little. You might find things aren't as heavy when you're not carrying them all by yourself."

Capri stared at the sunflower in her hand, blinking back tears.

Jake's words lingered, gentle and grounded, weaving through her doubts. She had spent so long convincing herself she was better off alone, that the weight of her life was hers to bear. But here he was, offering something she hadn't realized she needed—someone to stand beside her, to share the load.

Her father, her stepdad...even her mother had left her. But she didn't have to be alone. She could let Jake in and let things take its course. Yes, she could get hurt again, but the risk might be worth it.

Slowly, she lifted her gaze to meet his, the warmth in his

eyes undoing her last bit of resistance. Taking a breath, Capri stepped forward, closing the small space between them. She reached for his hand, her fingers lacing through his with calm certainty. "Let's see where this goes," she said softly, feeling her heart pound steady as if she were finally stepping into something she didn't need to control.

And as Jake's mouth slid onto hers, for the first time in a long while, she felt like she might be ready to stop running.

When he finally pulled back, Capri lifted her head, her fingers still entwined with his, feeling like that sunflower—turning slowly toward the sun, finding the courage to reach for the light despite the shadows behind her.

28

The sound of laughter and the clinking of glasses filled Capri's newly built patio as she carried a platter of deviled eggs to the rustic wooden table. The smell of pine and fresh-cut grass hung in the air, mingling with fresh raspberries plucked from her mother's patch. Capri had to admit, everything looked perfect out here, with the sun filtering through the trees and casting warm, dappled light across the new wooden planks.

Reva, Lila, and Charlie Grace sat around the table, their faces glowing in the soft afternoon sunlight. Capri smiled as she joined them, setting the deviled eggs down on the table, her excitement barely contained.

"Okay, Capri, you've been grinning like the cat that swallowed the canary all afternoon," Lila said, raising an eyebrow. "What's going on?"

Capri laughed, feeling the excitement bubble up inside her. "I might have some news to share," she said coyly, picking up one of the eggs and biting into it, savoring the moment.

Reva leaned in, her eyes narrowing playfully. "Spill it, Capri. We're dying over here."

Capri met Reva's gaze, then winked, her lips curling into a secret smile. "Well, you know how we talked about cracked eggs?"

Reva's eyes widened in realization, and a knowing smile tugged at the corners of her mouth. "Oh, really?" she teased, leaning back in her chair and crossing her arms. "So, you've decided to be okay with a few cracks?"

Capri nodded, uncertainty tightening her chest as the words slipped out. "Jake and I...we're moving forward. Slowly, but I'm not holding back anymore."

A chorus of squeals erupted from the table. Lila nearly knocked over her iced tea, and Charlie Grace reached across to grab Capri's hand, squeezing it tightly.

"Oh my gosh! Capri, this is huge!" Charlie Grace said, her eyes wide with excitement. "I didn't think you'd admit it, but look at you, all in love!"

Capri blushed. "I wouldn't go that far. But...I'm giving it an honest shot. Jake...well, he's different."

"Different in all the right ways, I bet," Lila added, her grin widening. "I'm so happy for you, Capri."

Reva, who had been silently watching the exchange, raised her glass of tea and smiled. "To moving forward, cracks and all," she said, her voice warm with pride.

Capri lifted her glass in return, her heart lighter than it had felt in a long time. They clinked glasses, the sun high in the sky, casting a bright glow over the patio. For the first time in what felt like forever, Capri wasn't looking over her shoulder at the past. She was finally stepping into the light—and it felt good.

As the happy conversation flowed around her, Capri leaned back in her chair, glancing at the new patio furniture Jake had surprised her with. She smiled to herself, realizing how much had changed in just a short time. Maybe things weren't perfect, maybe she wasn't perfect, but sitting here with her friends, with a future that didn't feel so frightening anymore, she couldn't help but feel hopeful.

And for now, that was enough.

The conversation slowed, and Reva straightened in her chair, her tone shifting. "I'm so happy for you, Capri. But while we're all together, there's something we need to talk about. You all know the government's mandate to retrofit the city buildings after the earthquake? Well, the town's finances are tight—really tight."

The joy in the air quieted as the weight of Reva's words settled over them.

"What are we talking about, Reva? How much is needed?" Charlie Grace asked, leaning forward.

Reva sighed, running her finger around the rim of her glass. "More than we've got. The estimates to bring the buildings up to safety standards are pretty staggering. The town doesn't have the funds, and if we don't figure something out, we're going to be stuck."

Capri frowned, feeling the reality of the situation hit hard. Thunder Mountain was a small town, and earthquakes weren't something they had prepared for. "So, what's the plan? Can we raise money for it?"

"I've been thinking," Reva began, tapping her fingers on the table. "We need something big. A community event that brings people together and raises enough awareness. Something unique."

Charlie Grace nodded. "You're thinking along the lines of a fundraiser?"

"Exactly," Reva said. "But not just any fundraiser. Something that would get the entire town talking and involved. Something that would gather interest beyond our tiny community and spark interest in donating to an online crowdfunding account."

Lila perked up, a slow smile forming on her face. "What about a Rocky Mountain oyster fry? It's different, it's local, and you know people's interest would perk up just for the novelty of it."

Capri's eyes widened. "You mean *real* Rocky Mountain oysters?" She stifled a laugh as the idea took shape. "Rocky Mountain oysters—only in Thunder Mountain would people line up for fried bull testicles without batting an eye."

Lila chuckled. "Why not? People love that sort of thing out here. We could sell tickets, have donated prizes for a raffle, and maybe even get some local businesses to sponsor."

Reva leaned back in her chair, her expression bright with excitement. "It might not cover everything we need, financially speaking, but it's a start. And if we can get the town excited about it, maybe more people will step up and donate to the fund."

Charlie Grace grinned. "I can already picture it—local businesses could donate items for the raffle, and we could get people from neighboring towns to come too. I'll reach out to a few ranches, see if we can get some contributions." She paused, an idea seeming to form. "I can ask Nick for ideas to get the word out. His production company has a whole marketing division."

Capri nodded, feeling a sense of hope filling the group despite the challenges ahead. "It won't be enough on its own, but if we can pull it off, it'll show the community is serious about getting this done. Maybe it'll inspire more people to help."

Reva smiled, her shoulders relaxing a little. "It's a start. That's all we can ask for right now. I'll send out an email about the mandate, detailing the requirements, and alerting residents of our plans."

The friends exchanged looks, the energy shifting back to

something hopeful. They knew the road ahead wouldn't be easy, and the fundraiser would only scratch the surface of what was needed. But for now, it felt good to have a plan—a way to move forward, just like Capri had with Jake.

29

T he four girlfriends stood in the town square, the faint scent of freshly baked bread and roasted coffee drifting over from the nearby Heavenly Bites Bakery. Capri adjusted her ball cap and eyed the list in Reva's hand. "Why do I feel like we're about to go to war?"

Charlie Grace laughed. "Because you've never been part of a fundraiser in Thunder Mountain before."

Reva, clipboard held like a shield, grinned. "Don't worry. With my mayoral charm, we'll have them eating out of our hands."

"Yeah, but will they be eating oysters?" Lila asked, eyeing the long list of businesses they had to hit.

Capri placed her hands on her hips. "If Gibbs Nichols is involved, they'll be washed down with beer. Charlie Grace's ex never passes up a cold one." She turned her cap backwards on her head. "Let's divide and conquer, ladies."

With determined nods, the girls split up, each armed with a list along with charm, determination, and, in Capri's case, a growing headache.

Minutes later, she pushed open the door to the Yarn Barn,

greeted by the familiar sound of knitting needles clicking. The Knit Wit ladies were gathered around their usual table, surrounded by skeins of brightly colored yarn.

Betty Dunning, the leader of the Knit Wit crew, looked up from her knitting, a spark of suspicion in her eyes. "Well, this is a surprise, Capri. What brings you by?"

"By now, you've probably received Reva's email about the earthquake remediation mandate."

All the ladies nodded their heads, followed by a chorus of "We sure did."

Capri grasped the opportunity to launch her pitch. "We're organizing a Rocky Mountain oyster fry to raise money for the earthquake retrofit. We could really use your help."

Betty pursed her lips. "And by help, you mean what exactly?"

Capri shrugged. "I don't know...maybe donate some knitted potholders? Or a few of those meat pies you made last year?"

Dorothy Vaughn, who was always game for anything, piped up. "We could do both! I'll throw in a couple of pies, though they'll be filled with peaches. My trees are loaded this summer."

"I'll bring some meat pies," offered Betty.

Capri raised a brow. "As long as they're not from whatever critter crawled into your shed this summer," she teased, but only slightly.

Betty cackled. "No promises."

Betty could be unpredictable when it came to her cooking. Last year's mystery stew still haunted Capri's taste buds. Betty laughed, the sound hearty and unapologetic.

"Oh, don't worry, honey," she quickly added with a wink. "This year, I'm sticking to beef. Well, mostly."

The group chuckled, but Capri shot a glance at Dorothy, who gave her a subtle shake of the head, silently warning her not to ask too many questions. When it came to Betty's culinary creations, sometimes ignorance really was bliss.

Next, Capri headed to Albie Barton's office. Albie was hunched over his typewriter, the sound of clacking keys filling the room.

"Albie, we need front-page coverage," Capri said, not wasting time on pleasantries.

"Let me guess, the fry." Albie didn't look up, still typing.

"We need to drum up excitement." She also told him about their idea for the online crowdfunding page and the need to publicize it.

Albie paused, finally glancing at her over his glasses. "I'll see what I can do. But remember, I have deadlines to meet. I'll need all the information pronto."

Capri rolled her eyes. "You write for the *Thunder Mountain Gazette*, not *The New York Times*."

He grinned, his hands hovering over the keys. "Fine, it'll go out in the morning. Front page. But I get to title it."

Capri groaned. "As long as it's not something ridiculous like 'A Calf's Biggest Sacrifice.'"

Albie thew his head back in laughter. "Now you're just giving me ideas."

REVA, Lila, and Charlie Grace were already at the Rustic Pine when Capri walked in. Pastor Pete, polishing glasses at the bar, raised a brow at their request.

"You want a donation?" Pete asked, the corners of his mouth lifting. "Sure thing! Annie and I will give you a couple of kegs, but only if you girls can beat me in a game of darts."

Reva groaned. "Pete, you know I've got about as much dart skill as a blindfolded cow."

"And I'm no better," Lila added. "None of us are very good at this."

Capri picked up a dart and eyed it confidently. "Speak for yourselves. I've been known to score a bullseye on occasion."

"Even so, I'm not sure this is a good idea," Reva said. "Capri may have talent, but the rest of us suck at darts." She pointed her finger at Pete. "I suspect you already realize you have little to worry about when it comes to this competition."

"That's why it's fun," Pastor Pete said, already pulling the darts from behind the bar. "Besides, the stakes are high—free beer."

Charlie Grace raised a brow. "What happens if we lose?"

Pastor Pete grinned. "You get the beer anyway. But I get to brag about it all week."

Reva shook her head, laughing as she grabbed a dart. "Alright, deal. But just know, we're only accepting this challenge for the sake of our beloved Thunder Mountain."

The girls took turns throwing, missing the board more than once, and Pastor Pete, true to form, didn't let them live it down. But in the end, they walked out with their kegs secured and a fresh story to tell.

"You do realize we're never going to hear the end of this, right?" Reva muttered as they left.

"Worth it," Capri said, smirking. "We've got our free beer."

CAPRI WANDERED over to the cemetery, knowing Oma would be there, sitting next to Earl's grave. As expected, the old woman was perched in her lawn chair with a fresh platter of cinnamon rolls.

"Afternoon, Oma," Capri greeted, pulling up a nearby stump. "We're getting donations for the fundraiser."

Oma's face lit up. "For the oyster fry?"

"Yup. Got anything you want to donate?"

"I'll donate a couple of batches of cinnamon rolls. They'll go faster than those oysters, I guarantee."

Capri grinned. "You're the best. Earl's lucky to have you keeping him company with rolls like these."

Oma laughed, offering one to Capri. "Have one for the road, dear."

The last stop was Wylie's Feed and Seed, where Wylie himself was fiddling with a display of lawn and garden equipment. When they asked for his contribution, he grinned.

"I'll donate," he said, scratching his beard. "But only if you make sure everyone knows it's my secret recipe for the oysters."

Capri smirked. "Your recipe? Since when do you know how to fry anything?"

"Trade secret," Wylie said with a wink.

Reva laughed. "We'll just put your name in lights then."

"Deal," Wylie said, shaking hands.

The sun was setting as the four of them gathered back at the town square, tired but satisfied. They plopped down on the steps of the Moose Chapel, reviewing the list of donations.

"Well," Reva said, scanning the paper. "This is a good start. We've got a keg, pies, cinnamon rolls, and...questionable meat pies."

Lila groaned. "Only in Thunder Mountain could we fundraise for an earthquake with Rocky Mountain oysters and mystery meat."

Capri smiled, leaning back against the steps. "If this town can survive this oyster fry, it can survive anything."

Charlie Grace chuckled. "Here's to the fry. Let's hope people come for the food and stay for the cause with checkbooks in hand."

"And the keg," Capri added, raising an imaginary glass. "Definitely the keg."

30

The day of the Rocky Mountain oyster fry dawned clear and crisp, the blue Wyoming sky stretching endlessly overhead, unmarred except for a single white jet trail cutting across the expanse, a silent reminder of life beyond Thunder Mountain. A light breeze fluttered through the town square outside the community center, carrying with it the distinct tang of frying oil and the earthy scent of freshly mown grass. Tables lined with checkered cloths stretched across the square, heaped with homemade pies, casseroles, and of course, platters of crispy fried Rocky Mountain oysters.

Capri stood off to the side, watching the crowd slowly grow as more townspeople trickled in. Kids darted around, weaving through the legs of adults carrying plates piled high with food. Laughter and conversation hummed in the background, blending with the distant music filtering out from the speakers Reva had set up near the makeshift stage.

Capri scanned the crowd, her eyes falling on Charlie Grace, who was laughing with some ranch hands from the guest ranch. She looked more relaxed than Capri had seen her in weeks. Maybe it was the success of the oyster fry—or maybe it was Nick Thatcher, who stood beside her, looking as rugged as ever in his jeans and worn boots, a baseball cap shielding his eyes from the sun.

Capri couldn't help but smirk. Who would've thought Charlie Grace would end up dating a big-shot production designer from Los Angeles?

As the smell of frying oysters thickened, Capri drifted closer to the food table, eyeing the thermometer display Reva had placed by the stage. A thick red line crept toward the top, but so far, the line was far from reaching their goal.

The donations had been pouring in all day, but despite the best efforts of the town, they were still short. She crossed her arms, feeling a knot of worry in her stomach. They had to make this work. The earthquake remediation mandate was breathing down their necks, and without enough money to retrofit the town's buildings, Thunder Mountain would be in serious trouble and subject to possible fines—let alone if a much bigger quake ever hit.

"You look like you're ready to wrestle a bear," Reva's voice pulled her from her thoughts. She stood beside Capri, holding a clipboard, her signature no-nonsense expression softening as she followed Capri's gaze to the donation thermometer. "We'll get there. People are still coming in."

Capri sighed. "I hope so. I don't know how much more we can do. The raffle's just about wrapped up, and we're still short."

Reva tilted her head, glancing around. The square was packed with townsfolk—familiar faces that had been there through the ups and downs of Thunder Mountain life. Oma, as always, sat in her lawn chair with a thermos of coffee by her side, a tray of cinnamon rolls perched precariously on her lap. The Knit Wit ladies were huddled together, knitting needles clicking as they chatted between bites of pie. Pastor Pete and his wife, Annie, were making the rounds, shaking hands and offering words of gratitude. Even Albie Barton, the town's newspaper reporter, was there, scribbling notes furiously as if the fry was the biggest event to hit the town in years.

Nicola Cavendish, Thunder Mountain's self-appointed gossip queen, stood near the donation booth, her tiny Yorkie, Sweetpea, yapping incessantly at passersby. Capri cringed as Nicola waved a hand dramatically, her husband Wooster standing beside her, looking as though he'd rather be anywhere else. Nicola's voice was loud enough to carry across the square, though anyone who knew her also knew that was part of the charm—or the curse, depending on the day.

"I heard Marjorie Pembroke's niece is moving back to town," Nicola announced, clutching Sweetpea under one arm as the little dog squirmed. "Word is she's fresh out of a nasty divorce. Wouldn't surprise me if she's after Mayor Reva's job next, mark my words!"

Capri caught Reva's eye from across the square, and the mayor just sighed, shaking her head with a resigned smile. "At least Nicola's consistent," Reva muttered as she approached Capri, nodding toward Nicola, who was now shoving a fried oyster into Wooster's mouth to quiet him. Poor man barely got a word in edgewise.

"Do you think her dog ever stops yapping?" Capri asked, stifling a laugh as Sweetpea let out another high-pitched bark.

"If Sweetpea's ever quiet, it's because Nicola's talking louder," Reva said dryly. "Though between the two of them, I'm not sure which one is more annoying."

Capri smirked. "I'd say it's a tie."

She glanced around at the crowd. "Still no sign of those TV people?" she asked, her eyes narrowing as she scanned the crowd for the Bear Country crew. She'd hoped their presence would bring in more donations, maybe even some publicity for their cause.

"Oh, they're around," Reva said, a slight smile playing on her lips. "Nick's already handed out flyers to his crew. They're probably stuffing their faces with oysters somewhere."

CAPRI RAISED A BROW, glancing at Charlie Grace and Nick again. The way Charlie Grace leaned into him, her hand resting on his arm, made Capri's face break into a pleased grin.

Her smile widened as she caught sight of Jake making his way toward her, a familiar warmth settling in her chest. The earlier uncertainty that had once held her back seemed like a distant memory now. She no longer fought against the pull she felt toward him; instead, she welcomed this new relationship and the way he made her all tingly inside.

As he drew closer, his eyes locked on hers, and a slow, easy grin spread across his face. It wasn't the kind of smile that demanded anything—just the kind that told her he was there, confident and sure, ready for whatever came next. She let her hands fall from her pockets and met him halfway, the sense of rightness in the moment undeniable. For the first time in a long while, she wasn't running from anything.

"Hey," she said, turning her cheek toward him.

"Hey, yourself," Jake whispered softly near her ear, his breath warm as he brushed a gentle kiss across her skin.

A sudden clatter drew their attention back to the food table, where Betty Dunning had knocked over a tray of her infamous meat pies. Capri stifled a laugh as Betty scrambled to gather them, her cheeks flushed with embarrassment. "I swear, these pies have a mind of their own," Betty muttered, brushing off crumbs with a huff. She shot a good-natured glare at the nearby kids giggling at the mishap, then straightened up, the pie tray in hand, as if nothing had happened.

Capri exchanged an amused glance with Reva, who shook her head with a grin. It was moments like this—little bits of chaos in the middle of something so community-driven—that reminded Capri why she loved this town.

Just then, Charlie Grace called out, waving them over. "Capri! Reva! You've gotta try these oysters! They're even better than last year."

Capri walked across the square with Jake by her side, their shoulders brushing as they moved through the lively crowd. The sun was warm on her skin, the air filled with the sounds of laughter, clinking dishes, and the sizzle of frying oysters. Jake nudged her with a smile, but her eyes were still drawn to the thermometer by the stage, the red line stubbornly stuck below their goal. Even as Charlie Grace handed them both plates of food, Capri's focus remained on that line, her thoughts swirling around the daunting gap they still needed to fill. Jake seemed to sense her tension, giving her a reassuring squeeze on the arm as if to say they'd figure it out, one way or another.

"Think we're going to make it?" Charlie Grace asked, her voice low, eyes also on the donation tracker.

"Not unless a miracle happens," Capri muttered, taking a bite of an oyster. "Everyone in town has rallied and given far beyond what is reasonable. We've done everything we can." She paused.

Charlie Grace opened her mouth to reply, but before she could speak, Nick stepped forward, his deep voice cutting through the noise. "We're short, huh?" he said, hands on his hips as he surveyed the scene.

Capri gave a brief nod. "We're still about eight thousand less than what we'd hoped to raise. Despite all the food, pies, beer, and raffles, we haven't managed to close the gap."

Nick glanced at Charlie Grace, a knowing smile passing between them. Then he turned, raising his voice so the crowd could hear. "I think we can fix that."

His words cut through the chatter, and suddenly all eyes were on him. He stepped onto the small stage where Reva had been making announcements earlier, and for a moment, Capri wasn't sure what he was about to do.

Nick cleared his throat, gripping the microphone with one hand, his other hand resting casually in his pocket. "I know how much this town means to Charlie Grace—and to everyone here. *Bear Country* has had the privilege of filming in this beautiful part of the world, and we know how important it is to preserve what makes Thunder Mountain special. So, on behalf of our production team, I'm making a donation to cover the rest of what's needed."

Gasps echoed through the crowd, and Capri's heart skipped a beat.

Reva stepped forward, wide-eyed. "Wait, you're serious?"

Nick nodded, his smile widening. "Every penny."

For a moment, there was stunned silence. Then the crowd erupted into cheers and applause, the sound reverberating off the old brick buildings that surrounded the square. Capri found herself grinning despite the knot of tension that had been coiled in her chest all day.

Charlie Grace beamed up at Nick, her face flushed with pride. She wrapped her arms around him, planting a quick kiss on his cheek as he chuckled, clearly enjoying the attention.

Capri caught Reva's eye, and they exchanged a look of relief. The fundraiser was a success. Thunder Mountain had pulled through once again.

As the applause died down, Nick handed the microphone to Reva, who smiled at him, her expression full of gratitude. "I don't think we can thank you enough, Nick."

Nick just shrugged. "It's the least we could do. Besides, you haven't seen the bill for all the food we've eaten yet."

The crowd laughed, and the atmosphere shifted, lighter and more relaxed now that the pressure was off. Capri stood back, watching as townsfolk mingled and laughed, a feeling of peace settling over her. The day wasn't just about the money raised—it was about the people. The town coming together, just as they always did, to support each other.

As she glanced back at the sky, the plane's white trail had faded, disappearing into the blue expanse. But here on the ground, Thunder Mountain's community stood strong, and for the first time in weeks, Capri felt like maybe things would be okay after all.

31

C apri stood at the threshold of her freshly renovated cabin, her heart doing a strange dance in her chest. The smell of wood polish lingered in the air, the sunlight streaming through the wide windows Jake had insisted on installing. Everything felt...new. The house, her life, her outlook—it was as if her world had been rebuilt brick by brick, just like these walls. She glanced around, and for the first time in what felt like forever, she let out a long, contented breath.

From behind her, she heard voices—a lot of them.

"Surprise!" her girlfriends yelled, spilling into the house with grins that reached their eyes. Reva, Charlie Grace, and Lila led the charge, arms loaded with balloons and trays of food. Behind them came a gaggle of familiar faces from town. The Knit Wit ladies, Pastor Pete and Annie, even old Albie Barton with his notebook, ready to jot down every juicy detail for the next issue of the *Thunder Mountain Gazette*.

Capri blinked, her mind catching up to the scene unfolding before her. "Wait, what—what is all this?"

Reva gave her a playful nudge. "A housewarming party, duh!

You didn't think we'd let you sneak by with a new house and no celebration, did you?"

Charlie Grace smirked, already making a beeline for the kitchen. "I brought deviled eggs, of course. And Clancy sent over that whiskey you like. If you're going to break in this place, you might as well do it right."

Capri shook her head, laughing. "You guys didn't have to do this."

"Of course we did," Lila chimed in, setting down a platter of cupcakes. "We've been with you through all the...tremors." She winked, and Capri couldn't help but chuckle at the inside joke. Earthquakes had shaken more than just the ground beneath them.

As more guests arrived, Capri's gaze traveled around the house. The walls had been stripped and rebuilt, just like her heart. The hardwood floors gleamed beneath her feet, strong and polished, a reminder that sometimes, the old had to be torn down to make space for something even better.

Jake stood by the fireplace, quietly observing the chaos of the surprise party with a smile tugging at his lips. He caught Capri's eye and grinned, his pride evident in the way his shoulders squared and his arms crossed, satisfied.

She walked over to him, heart fluttering. "You knew about this?"

He raised an eyebrow, feigning innocence. "Me? I'm just the guy who built the place."

She rolled her eyes, nudging him playfully. "Yeah, right."

Jake leaned down, his voice low. "I didn't build this alone, Capri. You've done just as much work here as I have...with both the house and your heart."

Capri stilled at his words. He always had a way of saying things that made her feel grounded and...seen. The once solid walls she'd kept around her heart had been dismantled, just like the old cinderblock foundation. She might still be afraid of losing control, but with Jake standing there, she realized she didn't have to control everything to be happy.

Before she could respond, a new wave of laughter and cheers erupted by the door. Capri turned to see her mother, looking more radiant than she'd seen her in years, stepping inside arm-in-arm with Earl.

"Mom?" Capri's eyes widened in surprise.

Her mom's gaze swept over the cabin, taking in the changes. "I like what you did to the place..." she said, pausing as her eyes drifted to Jake, "...and to your life."

Capri's heart warmed, the weight of her mother's words settling in. She stepped forward, hugging her tightly. "I like your new life too, Mom," she whispered with a wink at Earl, who beamed at her.

"Well, looks like we're both getting the hang of this whole 'letting go' thing, huh?" her mom said, pulling back with a watery smile.

"I guess so," Capri replied, feeling the truth of it down to her bones. Her friends, her mom, and Earl—they had all moved forward, embracing change, and now it was her turn.

Jake cleared his throat, stepping forward and offering a hand to Earl. "Glad you could make it, Earl."

Earl shook his hand with a firm grip, nodding approvingly. "Thanks for calling with your invitation. I see you've been taking good care of our girl here."

Capri's cheeks flushed, but she couldn't help the grin that tugged at her lips. "I'm still my own woman, Earl. But...he's doing okay."

Everyone laughed at that, and Capri felt the warmth of their love and support like a comforting blanket wrapped around her.

As the evening wore on, the house filled with chatter, laughter, and a sense of belonging that Capri hadn't realized she'd missed. Nicola Cavendish stopped by with Sweetpea in tow, gossiping loudly, while Bodhi West showed up with his girl-friend from Seattle, who looked both bewildered and amused by the town's eccentricities.

Nicola leaned in, her voice a stage whisper as she spoke to Bodhi. "I heard Mrs. Fuller's prize-winning roses mysteriously wilted overnight. Some folks are saying it's sabotage—probably Clara, still bitter about the bake-off," she said, with a knowing nod. "And did you see Frank Gray last week? New toupee if you ask me!"

As the party buzzed around them, Jake quietly disappeared for a moment and returned with a bouquet of sunflowers, their bright yellow petals glowing like miniature suns in his hands. He held them out to Capri, his gaze soft and full of meaning. "I thought these might suit you," he said, his voice low.

Capri's breath hitched as she took the flowers, the symbol of resilience and warmth—much like her journey with Jake. "They're perfect," she whispered, her heart swelling, knowing that like these sunflowers, she was glad she decided to turn toward the light.

At one point, Capri found herself standing at the edge of the patio—her new patio, complete with the furniture Jake had so sweetly bought, despite the initial panic it had caused. She ran her hand over the smooth wood of the railing, admiring the view of the Grand Tetons in the distance. Her life had been chaotic, wild, and at times terrifying, but it was also beautiful. Like the mountains, it had endured countless storms and still stood tall.

Jake came up beside her, slipping his arm around her waist. They stood in comfortable silence, watching the sun now drop lower in the sky, painting the tops of the Teton peaks in hues of pink and orange.

"I guess this is it, huh?" Capri murmured. "The end of our project."

Jake looked down at her, his eyes soft and full of that calm she'd come to depend on. "Not the end. Just the beginning."

Capri smiled at that. She rested her head against his shoulder, finally allowing herself to relax fully into his embrace. "I think I like that," she whispered.

Inside, she could hear her friends laughing, probably over some ridiculous thing Nicola had said, and her mom chatting with Reva about the latest town drama. The people she loved were all around her, in this house that now felt more like home than ever.

"I like what you did to the place," Jake said softly, echoing her mom's words from earlier.

Capri turned to him, eyes sparkling. "I couldn't have done it without you."

"You didn't have to," Jake replied, kissing the top of her head. "You just had to let me in."

And for the first time, Capri was okay with that. Letting someone in didn't mean losing control; it meant gaining something she hadn't realized she'd needed all along.

As the sky darkened and the stars began to twinkle above, the sound of her friends' laughter drifted through the open windows. Capri took another look around her new home—the walls sturdy, the floors solid, just like the foundation of the life she was finally ready to build with Jake.

And as Jake's hand found hers, their fingers intertwining, she knew with absolute certainty that this was just the beginning of a new, beautiful journey.

AUTHOR'S NOTE

Hello, Readers!

A heartfelt thank you for reading the Teton Mountain Series. These books celebrate the invaluable role of friendships. I am thankful to have girlfriends I've known since high school. These women bless me beyond what I can describe.

The spark for these stories was my own experiences of profound friendship, a theme I've always wanted to explore in my writing.

A trip to Yellowstone National Park and the Teton Mountain National Park in Wyoming inspired the setting. For any of you who have followed me, you know I thrill to take my readers to places I love to vacation. In these books, you'll be whisked away to the majestic Teton Mountains, you'll dine in the trendy restaurants in Jackson Hole, and see bears and moose in secluded pinewood forests. You'll experience herds of buffalo roaming the meadows of Hayden Valley and hike the backcountry trails around crystal blue lakes lined with pastel-colored lupine blooms. The town of Thunder Mountain is a fictionalized community based upon DuBois, Wyoming—a charming western town with wooden boardwalks and quaint buildings lining its Main Street. I took a little liberty as an author and relocated it to where Moran is now on the map.

Mostly, I created four women friends who have become so very dear to me as I've placed them on the pages of these books —Charlie Grace, Reva, Lila and Capri.

I hope you enjoy the time spent with us!

Kellie Coates Gilbert

ABOUT THE AUTHOR

USA Today Bestselling Author Kellie Coates Gilbert has won readers' hearts with her heartwarming and highly emotional stories about women and the relationships that define their lives. As a former legal investigator, Kellie brings a unique blend of insight and authenticity to her stories, ensuring that readers are hooked from the very first page.

In addition to garnering hundreds of five-star reviews,

Kellie has been described by RT Book Reviews as a "deft, crisp storyteller." Her books were featured as Barnes & Noble Top Shelf Picks and earned a coveted place on Library Journal's Best Book List.

Born and raised amidst the breathtaking beauty of Sun Valley, Idaho, Kellie draws inspiration from the vibrant landscapes of her youth, infusing her stories with a vivid sense of place. Kellie now lives with her husband of over thirty-five years in Dallas, where she spends most days by her pool drinking sweet tea and writing the stories of her heart.

Learn more about Kellie and her books at www.kelliecoatesgilbert.com

Enjoy special discounts by buying direct from Kellie at www.kelliecoatesgilbertbooks.com

Sign up for her newsletter and be the first to hear about new releases, sales, news, and VIP-only specials. Click here to sign up: VIP READER NEWS

WHERE TO FIND ME:

Kellie Coates Gilbert's Shop
(Enjoy special discounts!)

Kellie's Website: www.kelliecoatesgilbert.com

Gilbert Girls

(Facebook group)

ALSO BY KELLIE COATES GILBERT

Dear Readers,

Thank you for reading this story. If you'd like to read more of my books, please check out these series.

Purchase links found on my website:

www.kelliecoatesgilbert.com

TETON MOUNTAIN SERIES

Where We Belong – Book 1

Echoes of the Heart – Book 2

Holding the Dream – Book 3

As the Sun Rises – Book 4

MAUI ISLAND SERIES

Under the Maui Sky – Book 1

Silver Island Moon – Book 2

Tides of Paradise – Book 3

The Last Aloha – Book 4

Ohana Sunrise – Book 5

Sweet Plumeria Dawn – Book 6

Songs of the Rainbow – Book 7

Hibiscus Christmas – Book 8

PACIFIC BAY SERIES

Chances Are – Book 1

Remember Us – Book 2

Chasing Wind – Book 3

Between Rains – Book 4

SUN VALLEY SERIES

Sisters – Book 1

Heartbeats – Book 2

Changes – Book 3

Promises – Book 4

TEXAS GOLD COLLECTION

A Woman of Fortune – Book 1

Where Rivers Part – Book 2

A Reason to Stay – Book 3

What Matters Most – Book 4

STAND ALONE NOVELS:

Mother of Pearl

AVAILABLE AT ALL MAJOR RETAILERS

To purchase at special discounts:

www.kelliecoatesgilbertbooks.com

Made in the USA
Monee, IL
29 January 2025

11224675R10114